OUTLAWS

Shann was a planet without a sun. It was livable, but almost impossible to find—which made it a perfect rendezvous for the pirates and outlaws who infested the spaceways. Shann was also Vince Cullow's destination—and potentially his death-trap.

Colonel Vince Cullow of the Space Force was already dying—the first Earthman to have contracted a rare, non-terrestrial disease. But ironically, that made him the perfect man for a dangerous and vital mission: to stop the vicious Chullwei before their ruthless empire-building overran the galaxy.

Cullow's starting point: to infiltrate the force of Zarpi, an alien criminal ruled only by greed. His next step: to find Akorra, the brilliant female scientist who was somehow involved with Zarpi. His ultimate aim: to save the galaxy as well as his own life. And time was running out. . . .

SECRET OF THE SUNLESS WORLD

C. C. MacApp

A DELL BOOK

Published by
DELL PUBLISHING CO., INC.
750 Third Avenue
New York, New York 10017

SECRET
OF THE
SUNLESS
WORLD

CHAPTER ONE

ALMOST RUDELY, Major Vince Cullow declined the proffered arm. "Thank you, Nurse. I'm not so blind yet I can't walk down a flight of stairs without help." Nor, he thought rebelliously, old enough to be treated with solicitude by a pretty young girl.

Nevertheless he had to concentrate on the steps. Maybe, he thought, the uncertainty of his feet was another effect of the alien virus.

They reached the lower floor and turned down a long corridor that smelled of ether and isopropanol and more sophisticated medicines. Ashamed of his earlier tartness, he said to the nurse, "I thought they were more strict about visiting hours."

She said, a little conspiratorially, "It's a general, sir! They told me not to mention it in front of anyone else."

"Oh." What now, he wondered—more brass come to have a look at him before they sent him off to some isolated hospital to die? He supposed he *was* a prize exhibit—Earth's first spaceman to catch an alien disease.

"In here, sir." The nurse opened a door, stood aside for him to enter, and closed the door from the outside.

He peered at the figure seated by the neat, empty bed. "Tom! I thought you were on Pluto!"

Tom Fieser got to his feet and came forward, grinning, a hand thrust out. "I was. But the Nesse brought me home in one of their ships. From Pluto to Earth in twenty minutes!"

Vince blinked. Envy bit at him. "So they've finally

allowed an Earthman aboard! Did you learn anything? Are they going to—"

Fieser shook his head. "They were polite, but careful that I didn't see anything significant. I don't think they intend giving us the FTL in the foreseeable future." He stood looking at Vince with an odd expression. "Are the cataracts any worse?"

"Yes." Vince held his hand over his right eye and looked toward his friend. "I can barely recognize you. And the other eye's gone from 20/40 to 20/60. But that's not what drives me up the wall. The docs won't even talk about possible operations!"

"How about your skin? Anything odd showed up?"

Vince stared at his friend. "I thought that was supposed to be top secret. Well, yes. My skin feels tight around the face and neck. And I overheard a med tech say blotches show under a blue-light source."

Fieser said, "That'll get worse too."

Vince stood peering at the general for a minute, then slowly moved to the bed and sat down. "I see. Your coming here has something to do with the disease. Are there others who've got it?"

"No. No humans." Fieser moved directly in front of Vince. "Medicine is one thing the Nesse are willing to talk about. My M.O. on Pluto heard the reports of your infection—the initial fever and nausea and the beginning of cataracts, and the thing about the fingernails."

Vince automatically extended his hands for inspection. The nails were opaque white.

Fieser went on, "The Nesse know the disease. It's a virus loose in space that can infect most protein life. The eyes will get worse until you're completely blind, and your skin will get stiff and white. The virus seeks the light, once it's established. That's why it concentrates in the crystalline lenses of the eyes, among other places. What you have isn't the same as ordinary cataracts; it just looks the same." He paused and studied Vince. "If the disease runs its course it's fatal, Vince. In a year your internal organs will be immobile. The Nesse say the latter stages aren't pleasant."

Vince sat silent for a while. It wasn't any surprise to him—he'd known it, somehow. Anyway, to live on blind . . .

Sudden hope brought him to his feet. He took a step forward and grasped the other's biceps. "You said *if!* Can the Nesse cure it? *Will* they?"

Tom was oddly slow in answering. "No, Vince, they can't cure it. But they know someone who may be able to." He pulled away from Vince; walked to the single window and stared out at the too-orderly lawns and hedges for a minute, then turned. "Vince, I don't know how you're going to feel about this, but I can tell you *I'd* swap places with you in a split second. The Nesse *can* check the disease for a while. And they've made an offer. I'll have my tail in a crotch for coming to you without going through Top Command, but that'll pass. The offer is this: if you'll do a certain job for them, the Nesse will transport you to the place where you can be cured. They'll make all arrangements and pay all costs."

Vince stared stupidly. "You mean . . . somewhere, uh, somewhere *Out?*"

Tom Fieser grinned. "That's right. Out!" He punched Vince on an arm. "Ironical, isn't it? You and I and the rest were watched and hand-sorted so carefully; and now it turns out that *you*—because you're sick—can be the first human out of the solar system!"

Vince felt dizzy. For a moment he wondered if he were back in his room, asleep and dreaming. He knocked his knuckles against his thigh to make sure. "Why, hell! Of *course* I'll—what do you mean, you don't know how I'll feel? Why, I'll—I'll do anything they can think up! Any—" He broke off suddenly, took a deep breath, and sat down again. "Oh. Come to think of it, there are some things we wouldn't do, aren't there? If they expect—"

Tom shook his head vigorously. "The Nesse don't have any designs on the solar system, or on mankind; I'll bet my pension on that. To them, we're small potatoes. And they assure me they won't ask the slightest disloyalty to the human race. What they want of you is something unconnected with us. We just happen to have the right physical and mental equipment—and to be unknown except to them." He paused. "They admit they're interested in the medical angle too, but that's not the main thing." He paced a few steps. "You may never see Earth again, Vince, even if you get cured. They're frank about that. With what you'll learn, they may decide not to bring you back. Or, other things may happen to you. They don't minimize the dangers." He looked Vince in the eye fiercely. "How long do you want to think it over?"

"Think it over?" Vince laughed raggedly. "Don't be an ass, Tom! When can I go?"

CHAPTER TWO

LEOOR, skipper of the Nessen ship, was tall for his race, and that put him close to Vince's five-eleven. His age was hard to guess, as the hair of the Nesse was white to begin with. That hair was a jolt, seeing it for the first time. It was short and kinky so that it looked like a knit garment of some sort, completely covering the head, face, and what Vince could see of the body. Even the small round ears had their covering of curly down. The facial hair, though it grew thick, was dainty. The eyes were very pale, just tinted with blue, and a bit startling because they were much longer than a man's, running from the rather narrow bridge of the nose (which was long and slender) to the edges of the broad cheeks. Except for the broadness across the cheeks, the face was delicate, with a small mouth. The forehead seemed ample, though the facial hair made it hard to judge precisely what was forehead and what was scalp.

The Nesse were not a bulky species. Beside Vince (who, in spite of his disease, held the same weight he'd had as an Academy halfback) Leoor looked frail. But tendons stood out through the white fur, and the slender fingers looked hard and capable.

All in all, once he got used to Leoor, Vince liked him.

Leoor's manner, like his one-piece, zippered, thin white uniform, was unpretentious. His smile consisted of a tiny quirk of the mouth, plus a blinking of the long eyes. He spoke English well, with little accent, but of course with a trace of awkwardness. "We will leave the solar system in about two hours. Until then, please forgive my restrict-

11

ing you to certain parts of the ship. Later you will be free to move about it."

"Of course." Vince, no longer tempted to stare at the alien, peered about his assigned compartment, which held a bed, two chairs, a chest of drawers with a small mirror, and a piece of furniture—closed now—that might be a record player or a video set or both. The two doors in the wall away from the corridor might hide a bath and a kitchenette. "Uh, I don't notice any difference in the air. Ness must be a planet very much like Earth."

Leoor's mouth quirked. "Our air is a little thicker and a little higher in oxygen. However, we of this small force visiting your system have adapted to Earth's air, since we are privileged to land there occasionally. Your temperature control for this room is in the kitchenette. You can set it, and the humidity, to suit yourself; and there is a full range of lighting."

Vince had already noticed the luminous ceiling. He stood awkwardly for a minute, then, as his host seemed in no hurry to leave, walked to one of the chairs. "I suppose I might ask you to sit down. I, uh, guess I'll be pretty ignorant of your customs for a while."

Leoor lowered himself into the other chair. "There is little about our customs you will find strange. One of the reasons we decided to contact your race is that your mores and beliefs are close to our own. It is not so with all the advanced races in this cell of the galaxy."

Vince wondered about the word "cell," but didn't ask what Leoor meant by it. "Yes. Tom Fieser explained that our races have much in common. He said it was a factor also in your . . . well, deciding to hire me for whatever it is you want."

Leoor blinked twice, which seemed to be the equivalent of a nod. "A factor, yes. So far as you individually are concerned there is more. We had already discussed the hiring of a human, and wondered what might be a suitable payment. When we heard of your virus infection, we saw that we had something of great value to offer—at not too great a cost to us." The small mouth quirked. "We are bargainers, you see, like yourselves."

Vince grinned. Until he'd met Leoor, he'd wondered how Tom Fieser could trust the Nesse so completely. But if Leoor had any duplicity in him, it didn't show.

The alien skipper went on, "It is a delicate matter we wish you to help us with, involving a criminal of our own species, but also other races. That your kind is as yet unknown in this cell makes our task less difficult.

As Leoor paused, Vince took the opportunity to ask, "Excuse me—but what do you mean by 'this cell'?"

Leoor made an odd gesture, a flick of the fingers. "That is a matter of physics you will be studying while we travel. I could not explain simply now, but it is as if regular volumes of the galaxy, and of all space, are walled off from each other. The cell which includes your sun and ours is mostly well explored, but no one knows how to pass out of it to other cells. Forgive me for not elaborating."

"Of course," Vince said doubtfully.

Leoor went on, "Because your species is not so different from ours, we feel you may, if we can be forgiven the assumption, feel more friendly than if we were very different."

Vince nodded. "I don't think that's an unnatural assumption."

Leoor smiled his minimal smile. "Thank you. There is another reason we hope for your friendship. Sol lies in a part of the cell where, some time soon, a certain species with expansionist policies is likely to appear. A non-humanoid species—one with technology no further advanced than that of my people, but an empire of sufficient strength to be a formidable enemy. They—the Chullwei—would find the solar system, because of its location and raw materials, a very desirable acquisition." Again, the smile. "So you see, Major Cullow, that we assault you with inducements both personal and patriotic. By helping us you may help stave off the conquest of your system."

Vince, staring at the alien, felt himself flush. "I appreciate your frankness, and I've already agreed to whatever it is you want of me, with certain obvious reservations. What concerns me now is whether I'll stay alive long enough to keep the agreement. And whether I'll have eyesight to work with."

Leoor made a hesitant gesture with his left hand. "If I could give you complete assurance I would do so. I can only say that, in my own race, the same affliction can be and has been cured. Not by our own doctors, unfortunately. They can slow the progress for a while; and they tell me, with their usual hedging and counter-hedging, that your metabolism is very similar to ours. Here is what we *can* do. By a devious route we will send you to a place where the treatment is available. It is no coincidence that it is also the place where you may be able to perform a service for us. Or at least make the start." He sighed, very humanly. "It is not a gentle place, though there is great technology available there. It is, in fact, a supply center for outlaws—as well as an occasional fencing-ground of agents of legitimate powers momentarily engaged in illicit or clandestine activities." He quirked his smile. "Yes, Major Cullow, space—our cell of it at least—is full of intrigue. There are empires and rivalries and treacheries, and sometimes small wars which we try very hard to keep small. There are outlaws and pirates. There are strange races and weird customs and incomprehensible technologies. And into this hodgepodge we are going to drop you."

Vince was silent, dazed, for a while. Finally he said a trifle sourly, "Great. A secret agent! How long will I be booking up before I start sparring with other secret agents?"

Leoor smiled. "You will not have to do that, we hope. And you will not go into action unbriefed; we will be en route for some months, Terran time. Meanwhile, here are the basic facts: an ancient artifact of a great, long-vanished empire has been stolen from us. It may be the key to vast knowledge and power. One of our most respected scientists, a specialist in the archeology of that vanished empire,

14

has been kidnapped. We have ways of knowing that an out-law of my own race is responsible. He has in the past dealt with the Chullwei, and we fear he is doing so again. The point of contact, of course, is the place where you are going."

Vince sighed. "And just where is that? May I know?"

Leoor said, "The absolute truth is that *I* do not know. It is called Port-Of-Shann. Shann is a world without a sun, a self-warmed world whose location is a well-kept secret. Its proprietors—not native there—are called the Vred. They are not humanoid." Leoor smiled his smile. "So long as I am throwing names at you, the outlaw we seek is called Zarpi. The kidnapped scientist—a female of our species—is Akorra. Another outlaw, definitely not humanoid, who will take you to Shann, is named Gondal. His race are called Onsians." Leoor's long eyes rested on Vince's face for a minute. "And the ancient vanished people—whose importance you will understand when you begin to study—were the Lenj. The language of my own people, which you will learn, is Lenjan. Lenjan is the nearest thing to a universal language that exists in our cell." The Nessen officer got to his feet. "I will let you rest now. A doctor will come soon to see what he can do about checking that disease of yours."

CHAPTER THREE

VINCE, finishing lunch in his kitchenette, walked back to the chair he'd gotten so tired of sitting in during the last four-hundred-odd hours. He lowered himself into it, grumbling a little because his hip was very lame from the most recent hypodermic needle. He had to admit, though, that his virus disease didn't seem to be getting any worse.

He'd learned the language of his hosts (pure Lenjan, they said) well enough now to listen to recorded lectures. Today he was going to get a dose of archeology.

He pressed a stud under one arm of the chair, and the piece of furniture he'd first taken for a video set emitted a sort of grunt, opened its doors, and rolled across the slightly resilient floor to position itself in front of his chair. A picture glowed to life.

The elderly Nessen scientist who peered from the image was amusingly like his Terran counterparts. Except, Vince thought, he didn't have a beard. Nesse couldn't grow them.

The voice was didactic with a note of affected dry humor. "I am, as some of you know, Professor Nookore. The lecture I am about to deliver—I hope you don't find it as tedious as I do after delivering it some two hundred times—is requiring listening for Third Level School candidates. You need not takes notes. A printed summary is available." The professor paused, with a squeezing shut of his long eyes to signify humor, and pretended to shuffle through some papers.

"The Lenj." The wrinkled face peered owlishly from the

screen. "From infancy on, we hear that word. But we must not let familiarity dull its meaning." A forefinger rose admonishingly. "It is no mere truism to say that none of the high civilizations now existent can disavow the heritage of the Lenj. Consider the item of language alone. How many thousands of years would have elapsed before we evolved on our own a language of such utility? That, young people, is a legacy often underestimated. Language, spoken and written. A thing of even greater importance than the scraps of Lenjan technology we have dug up!" The lecturer paused and swept his presumed audience with a firm look.

Vince twisted impatiently in his chair. He wished the old clown would stop posturing and get on with the facts.

But the savant chose to sigh meaningfully. "How generous they were in scattering those scraps of technology. And how careful that their language be preserved, even to exact pronunciations—as if, in some inscrutable future, they intended to return. But how carefully they limited their gifts of technology, withholding certain things from us. Yes, that was surely deliberate.

"We know that their departure was hasty, for we have found many things they did not intentionally leave for us. We know there were battles—have you not heard almost as much about the Ancient Enemy as about the Lenj themselves? And the deep-buried wreckage is there for the finding.

"Yet, for all their haste, they took time to conceal two things above all: where they went, and how they left this cell. Clearly—though the Ancient Enemy has vanished as mysteriously as the Lenj—the Lenj feared pursuit.

"Many of you have seen one of the standard voice-reproducers they scattered on so many then-primitive worlds. But for the sake of those who have not, I will demonstrate one." The old hands lifted a small cylindrical device that made Vince think of a can of foam-type shaving cream. "It's entirely mechanical—you twist the base of it, so, and the voice emerges—and of such materials

17

and construction that thousands of them have lasted through the eons, through the quakes and floods and volcanoes that most planets know. What you will hear is the voice of a Lenjan dead, we estimate, some eleven thousand Nessen years." The lecturer gave the object a twist.

The voice was deep, rich, of a much firmer timber than the lecturer's. It recited simple multiplication tables and compass points, to yield, no doubt, some basic knowledge along with pronunciation.

The lecturer laid the device aside. "We know, of course, that the Lenj were not native to this cell. Neither, in all likelihood, were their enemies; for there is no sign that the latter dwelt long in this cell. The Lenj were here, as you know, for many generations—long enough to build a great empire, though not one of tyranny nor conquest. They taught, they traded, they helped.

"And now we consider a question so many have asked —will they ever return? The consensus among serious students is negative. So much time has passed. Almost certainly they are long vanished from the galaxy. Either their enemy, or some other catastrophe, overtook them.

"For mortal races do not survive forever; and the Lenj were not gods. There are ample hints they were all too mortal. Consider the matter of mythology, for instance— great scientists though they were, there appears to have been superstition among them. Consider, for instance, one scrap of their mythology recently uncovered. It reads: 'Wolami lazes beneath his lamp. When the lamp is extinguished, then will Wolami gird for battle.'

"This legendary god, or warrior-hero, is mentioned in other places, though only in passing. Nevertheless, they did—"

Vince, with a growl, jabbed at the chair-arm stud to turn the lecture off. It was hard enough to sit still and listen to *any* lecture; but when the lecturer maundered on about mythology. . . . He got to his feet, cursing at the soreness in his hip. He thought he'd wander about the ship for a while. Later, he'd try another of the tapes stacked up for him.

"Cellular nature of the universe."

This lecturer was younger, and delivered his talk flatly, without trying to amuse his listeners. Vince leaned forward, determined to hear it out no matter how boring it became.

"It is not to be thought," the dry voice went on, "that the cellular nature of space is a thing that affects ordinary physical movement at slower-than-light speeds, or at the speed of light itself. Thus, we see via straight lines the most distant stars of our own galaxy and others. Neither is the Milky Way disturbed in its vast slow whirl about our galaxy's center of gravity. It is only in the realm of faster-than-light travel that the cellular peculiarity shows itself." The lecturer paused long enough to fill his Nessen lungs. "Theory is that the pheomenon is related to the little-understood nature of FTL translocation from one point to another, rather than to any real property of space. As you know, FTL travel, including the extremely complex navigational problems, is a technology recovered only slowly and laboriously by our species and others. The Lenj may or may not have intended us to master it, but they did not make it easy. Nor so far, do we have any encouragement that we can ever unravel the secrets of their travel between cells.

"The limitations of ordinary FTL have been demonstrated dramatically and often. Ships have struck out into the unknown, trying new and sometimes fanciful navigational theories. Some, after incomprehensible shifts of course, have found themselves back in known areas of our cell. Others have never been heard from. Perhaps they met disaster within the cell. Or, if they did succeed in leaving the cell, and sent messages back via radio or some other electromagnetic media, those messages may still reach us centuries from now! The only way to get word back fast would be for the ship to retrace its path or to send a message-drone back along it via FTL."

Vince, striving to listen, found his mind trying to slide off into thoughts of his own future. If he regained enough health on Shann to continue with his project, he was supposed to notify Leoor—who was now removed from the Solar System Task Force and assigned to work with Vince. He was to report further if the outlaw Zarpi, or the female scientist Akorra, turned up there. He wondered, now, by what means he'd be expected to report. A message-drone was a miniature ship, with its own FTL drives and navigational computers. The ones he'd seen were four feet long—certainly no gadget for a spy to smuggle around in his shaving kit! He decided he'd ask Leoor as soon as this lecture was finished.

The Nessen skipper blinked a smile. "I've been wondering when you'd ask. Vince, there are odd bits of Lenjan technology being recovered from time to time. Some of them we keep secret." The white-furred alien got up from his desk, went to what looked like an ordinary combination wall-safe, and spun a dial with each hand. A circular door swung open. Leoor came back to the desk with several objects, laid them down for Vince's inspection, and opened a desk drawer to take out a magnifying glass. "I think you'll need this."

Vince peered through the glass at a dollar-sized disk with one flat edge.

"That," Leoor told him, "is one type of Lenjan power-unit. We call them 'Lenj coins'. Note the thin rim all around, and the deeply hollowed middle. If I had another one to put against it, you'd see a fascinating thing—you'd have to hold them very tightly to keep them together, and to prevent their turning until the flats were at least twenty degrees out of line. A peculiar variation of magnetism that a Lenj coin retains even when it's not charged." Leoor hefted the thing lovingly. "To activate it, you store it in hydrogen gas at two atmospheres for a couple of hundred hours. Then you have a very potent unit, but only in combination with one or more others like it. This coin is of an alloy, palladium and other metals, that absorbs hydrogen in considerable amounts and somehow transforms most of it to deuterium and tritium, the active isotopes. Press two activated coins together with the flat edges aligned, and you have a small atomic pile, not a really violent one. Force six together quickly—for instance, by ramming them into a suitably shaped tube—and you could blow this ship to particles!"

Vince involuntarily drew his hand away from the coin. Leoor smiled. "There's no hydrogen in it now."

Vince grinned sheepishly. "All right, so it's a sort of uncharged battery. How does it help me communicate with you from Shann?"

"It doesn't—that's a different thing. First, about these coins. We're giving you ten of them to take with you. They're rare, but not so rare that putting them up for sale on Shann would be an incredible thing. Tremendous wealth passes through Port-Of-Shann—or stays there. We think they may particularly interest Zarpi for another reason, and may be your entry into his acquaintance."

Vince shrugged and glanced at a wallet-like thing Leoor had brought from the safe. "Speaking of entries, is that a passport, or something?"

Leoor smiled again. "Good guess. It's passport, identification card, and credit card—ostensibly." He opened it. "Here's your picture. Can you read what's under it?"

Vince frowned at the peculiar script. "Why, it's Onsian, not Lenjan." He mumbled over it. "Vinz . . . Kul . . . Lo. It's my name, more or less!"

"Right. You're a pirate from a tenuously known region of our cell. Your connection is through Onsi, a remote planet. But this is something more—it's the communicator you asked about."

"Huh?"

Leoor smiled and ran a thumbnail around the edge of the photograph. "It comes out—See? There's only a small demi-magnetic force holding it in. Now—take it and turn it ninety degrees, put it back in place, and apply pressure to the refolded wallet. Sitting on it will do. There's a built-in power source that will send a message via the same path a ship or message-drone would take. We'll hear it. The message, when you've turned the picture ninety degrees clockwise, is 'Healthy and free!' Turn it another ninety degrees, and the message is, 'Zarpi here'. Three-quarters of a turn means, 'Akorra here'. Do you have it?"

Vince nodded. "I guess this is one of the secret bits of technology you mentioned. I won't need a message-drone, then."

"No, unless you have to send more detailed messages. That, you'll have to work out for yourself—with Gondal's help, possibly, if he's still there and if you can devise some way of disguising the messages. We wouldn't want to trust Gondal too far; he's a complete pirate."

Vince shrugged. "I suppose there's no use in my worrying about that now. What's this thing? He picked up what looked like a six-times-life-size plastic model of the Lenj coin.

"That," Leoor told him in a slightly tense voice, "is a replica of the artifact Zarpi stole. As you can see, it's identical in shape with the small coin—except that it has a slot in the flat edge, into which the coin will fit." The Nessen demonstrated. "The coin, if it were activated, would power something in the artifact. We don't know what the artifact was—the people who owned it were damnably uncooperative, and my government was too squeamish to seize it for study. We suspect it's a key of some kind; there are such things described in old treatises. I don't mean an ordinary key to an ordinary lock—I mean something that may or may not open a door or gate somewhere, but in addition is some kind of a programming unit for a Lenjan computer or computerized mechanism. We're dealing in hints and guesses. Akorra's specialty is Lenjan artifacts, though she's a fine physicist. Zarpi's had her kidnapped, and has stolen the artifact. And, of course, Shann figures in it somehow." He paused and eyed Vince seriously. "You can deduce as much from those circumstances as we can."

Vince, midriff tightening a little, thought it over. "I see. When are we meeting Gondal?"

"We'll be enroute to the rendezvous for another eighty hours. We have a message-drone saying he's already there, waiting."

CHAPTER FOUR

VINCE, annoyed at his own tense trembling, shook hands with Leoor in the two-handed Nessen way, picked up his two small valises, and followed a pilot toward a side port. He bent to squeeze into the shuttleboat, stowed the two bags under a bench, and sat down on it. There were no such things as bucket seats or belts; the boat, like the Nessen ship, had its own artificial gravity that compensated automatically for any acceleration.

The lights went dim.

He felt the slight jars as they uncoupled from the ship. There was no further sensation until metal curtains drew aside from the blunt forward end of the boat and revealed the stars.

He stared past the pilot at the unfamiliar constellation. Earth's fledgling ventures had made him familiar with the look of space, and from the solar system he'd had at least a feeling of acquaintance with the stars. Here, they were strangers. The hollowness inside him worsened, as he realized how far he was from home.

The boat seemed suspended, motionless. Perhaps fifteen minutes passed; then the pilot was murmuring something from his throat mike, and a tiny chime sounded. The pilot glanced back at Vince then pointed ahead. Vince, cursing his poor eyesight, peered in that direction.

It was just a tight cluster of lights at first, then he saw the pattern of them: a central circle with four strings running straight out from it to form a cross. The whole conglomeration swelled swiftly, and now there was the sensation that the boat was hurtling toward something. (Or vice versa, he reminded himself.)

There were sudden reflection-points of light on the transparent plastmetal of the boat's curved front window as the boat's searchlight came on. And, as the powerful beam lit the object ahead, he saw that it was a ship—not a single-hulled one like the Nessen vessel. There was one great middle hull like a giant milk can, with slender arms projecting out; and at the end of each arm, a much smaller hull. Presently he could see the ring of shiny concave surfaces on the flat end of the central hull, forming the typical external force-pans of an FTL drive. He'd learned a little about that by now. Then he saw that each of the smaller hulls was similarly equipped.

Each, then, was a ship in itself, tiny compared to the central one, yet bigger than anything Earth had built so far.

Finally he saw, nestled beside one of the four smaller hulls at the ends of their "arms" (which were mooring-columns, of course), a still smaller craft that looked more like the classical concept of a spaceship. It was long and slender and streamlined, with bumps and protuberances and a tripod set of landing-legs.

The shuttleboat, though he felt no deceleration, had slowed now, until they barely crept toward that slim streamlined ship. Presently he was able to judge that as about two hundred feet long—which made the middle hull of the alien ship a huge, squat cylinder a thousand feet in diameter! Now he saw the coupling-hatch in the side of the slim ship, lit in a way that clearly indicated they were to join onto it. The metal shields slid over the shuttleboat's window. He felt the coupling-on, heard a tiny whisper that was air pressure being equalized, then the boat's hatch slid open.

Vince stared into a dimly lit well that seemed to go to the core of the ship. Conscious of the pilot's amused eyes, he nodded a good-bye and thank you, picked up his bags, and moved toward the opening.

The pilot said suddenly, "Watch gravity!"

Vince, understanding, poked one of his bags ahead experimentally. As soon as it left the boat's limits it went weightless (though it still had, of course, inertia). Warned, he went through carefully and located handholds in the ship's lock.

The two intervening hatches closed, and Vince was apparently alone in the strange ship. Then a voice, sibilant and slow, but speaking fluent Lenjan, came from the intercom in the lock. "You are agile enough, I see. I was told you were half-blind." There was a moment of strange staccato hissing. "I was worried that you would be feeble, or that the boat would not make a tight couple for transfer. I would not like to lose a valuable cargo at the very outset! Hiss-hiss-hiss." There was a pause, then: "Come to the central corridor, then forward. I am in the control room, where I have turned on moderate gravity."

Vince, spine prickling, hesitated. "Who are you?"

Again the staccato hissing, which might be the equivalent of a chuckle. "I am Gondal, of course. Do you think I would leave a matter of such delicacy to a subordinate, who might begin to scheme on his own?"

Vince picked up the valises and hauled himself toward the fore-and-aft corridor, then along it toward a lighted doorway.

His first horrified impression was of big snakes growing out of a bulbous central body at least five feet in diameter. Then, as he clung there at the hatch of the control room, his eyes straining to focus in the free-fall, he saw that there were only two snakelike heads. There were also four tentacles sprouting from the upper part of the body, each ending in a pair of tapered digits. There was yet another sinuous thing, growing between the two thick snakelike necks, that was more than six feet long but only two inches thick. Hose-like, it was attached by some sort of mouth to a metal cannister strapped atop the bulging body.

Below the body were four thicker, shorter tentacles, each ending in two strong, flexible toes. One of the four leg-tentacles was curled around the stem of a pilot's seat, anchoring the creature. The other four were sprawled carelessly.

Gradually, he noted detail.

The skin was mottled, dark-and-lighter green, with obvious scars here and there. The snakelike heads had two eyes each, but only small braincases. The fangs were more like a wolf's than a snake's.

A spot between the topside appendages was swelling slowly. Vince realized the creature was inhaling from the cannister via the hose-like appendage. The four eyes regarded him, one pair remaining on his face while the other roamed up and down him. He got the impression that the principal brain was somewhere in the central body.

The hose-like thing separated itself from the air-tank, coiled, and poked its tip toward him. The staccato sound, which he was sure now must be a laugh, emerged from the nearly closed tip. He became aware of a faint smell of ammonia. Then came the slow speech. "Well, enter! I do not eat such valuable cargo. At least, not unless I am starving—which I am not now."

Vince, instincts screaming, maneuvered himself through the hatch. Gravity of about half a G tugged at him. He got his feet on the deck and stood struggling with his sense of nightmare.

The creature hissed. "I must hurry and teach you the controls of this quaint ship so I can get back to my own. I can breath your air, but I find it annoying. And I am tired of breathing from this can, which, by the smell, has recently been misused by one of my accursed crew. Hiss-hiss! How, again, are you named?"

"Uh—Vince Cullow."

"Vinz Kul Lo. Not too outlandish." A tentacle-tip writhed up and flicked a switch on an instrument-jammed panel. Hums and whines began somewhere in the ship. "Main power switch." The four leg-tentacles moved fluidly; whirled the big body about and hoisted it onto the pilot's seat, where it perched improbably. Topside tentacles flickered over the panel. "Grav drive master switch. Here, the controls for your three jets on the fins—a primitive means of propulsion but one that makes maneuvering possible without electronic detection. You do not, by the way, have gyros for turning this ship. This bank of switches and studs—ungodly arrangement!—is the internal control system: air conditioning, hatches, artificial gravity, lights, hoists, weapons and such." A tentacle flashed to another panel dominated by a large switch with a stud below it. "Master switch for the FTL drive—installed makeshift long after the ship was built. Your FTL is knocked out, which will be one excuse for taking you to Shann, where it can be repaired." A snakehead swept low over a keyboard. "Main computer. The last owner did some improving, so that you can program any of the controls through it. She is not such a bad old tub as she looks—or will not be, when the FTL is repaired. That will be finished by the time your eyes are made well." Gondal twisted himself out of the seat like some huge impossible rubber toy. "Come, sit here. You can practice by nestling us in behind the middle of my ship." The breathing-appendage went back to the cannister again.

Vince, dazed, moved unsteadily toward the seat. "Uh . . . Am I to understand that this is supposed to be *my* ship?"

A snakehead waved at him. "Of course! What kind of pirate would you be without a ship? And this is ideal; she's so old, and from such a remote world, that she cannot be traced!"

Vince slowly got into the seat and peered helplessly at the controls. A tentacle slid past him, smelling faintly of ammonia, and flipped a switch, bringing to life a one-foot-square view-screen with dim images on it. Then the labored voice said, "Oh, I forgot—your eyes." The tentacle did something and the view brightened.

The screen showed a side image of the huge central hull, with part of one mooring-arm foreshortened and slanting out of view. Gondal said, "Grav grapples are off. Take us out five hundred feet, a few thousand to the rear, then move up and touch the nose to the rear of my main hull. The crew will grapple you there."

Vince swallowed hard. I'll be damned, he thought, if I'll let him think humans are morons. He tried very hard to recall what the alien had just taught him.

The system, in general, was simple enough. There were studs with the Lenjan symbols for "rearward" and "forward," toggle-switches beside them large enough to be grasped by the hand. One trio of toggles was marked with simple numbers, one, two, three. Those must be drives in the landing-legs. Puzzling things out desperately, he recognized a symbol for "lateral."

Taking a deep breath, he chose toggles and pushed them very gently in what he thought was the right direction.

Acceleration tugged briefly at him before the ship's imperfect compensators reacted. Gondal hissed with huge amusement. "I said five hundred feet, not five hundred miles!"

Vince, face burning, experimented cautiously. Presently he had some mastery of things. He maneuvered the ancient craft to rearward of Gondal's huge ship, then, cautiously, edged in, trying to center himself between the FTL drive-plates. His pulse quickened. This was great! What delicacy of control he had, once he'd practiced a little!

A few feet from the huge hull they were suddenly stopped as if they'd rammed into a wall. Inertia forced him forward. Gondal hissed uproariously. "My timid hatchling-eaters of a crew! They've been listening in, and feared you'd blunder right inside!" Gondal swiped at a switch and roared thunderously into a microphone.

Imprecations equally rough came over the receiver. But the huge ship's grapple-forces took hold gently of the smaller vessel and eased her in until she nosed without impact against the great hull.

Moments later Vince felt something couple onto the captive ship. A shuttleboat, he supposed, arriving to take Gondal off. The Onsian confirmed that by heaving himself toward the hatch. "Dry-practice and study. There are things programmed into the computer for you to listen to. I must take a roundabout course to Shann. By the time we are there you must be familiar with this ship and your assumed role. Personally, I do not find you a convincing pirate—too honest of face. Hiss-hiss-hiss! But we will try. Call me if you have trouble."

"Uh . . . all right. Vince went to the hatch and watched the Onsian surge lithely down the corridor.

When he was alone in the ship, he explored a bit. There was plenty of food aboard, strange but palatable: meat of some kind, more like chicken than beef; packaged bread with an anise-like taste; fruits, more or less globular in shape; something not too unlike coffee; some plastic jars of a sort of beer; and a prudent range of seasonings that must have been sent in advance by the Nesse—salt, pepper, onion powder, and sugar.

There were indeed things for him to learn in the computer. He learned that Shann was slightly bigger than Earth but with gravity about equal; that its atmosphere was slightly higher in carbon dioxide, with an odd assortment of rare gasses; that Shann was indeed self-warmed by interior heat, which gave rise to peculiarities such as seas that boiled in spots, flora and fauna that produced dim lighting of their own or gathered around active volcanoes or that had very sensitive night vision, as well as keen hearing and smell. The weather seemed surprisingly like Earth's. Perhaps warmer and cooler areas, caused by varying thickness of the crust, created winds and rain.

From the description of the Vreddan proprietors, he pictured them as something between large canines and humanoids, walking upright. They ran the place with a limited but strict set of rules: outlaws of any stripe were welcome if they could pay, but must be on their good behavior. There were inns and cabarets, and businesses catering to a broad spectrum of needs. Several establishments maintained special environments for guests unable to breathe the planet's air.

There were repair facilities for any kind of ship.

And banks! Finance, it seemed, was the principal industry. The total of outlaw loot in safekeeping on Shann was beyond estimation. Gondal, recording the information, had mentioned the treasury with a note of wistful greed.

Time passed, and began to drag. Eventually, though, the moment came when Gondal's two snakeheads appeared on a screen. "Erase everything from the computers. I and several of my crew will come aboard soon to await the arrival of Vreddan inspectors."

"Then we're near Shann?"

"Timewise, quite near—though we must pause at some distance until we are cleared. I come, now."

The crewmen were little different from Gondal, slightly less rugged with fewer scars. Each wore weapons: pistols of two kinds, one obviously a beamer, the other possibly a pellet-firing gun. The grips were tubular and set at an obtuse angle to the barrels. The crewmen, after a curious scrutiny of Vince, left, hissing and grunting to each other in Onsian, and took up stations elsewhere in the ship. Gondal remained, taking occasional drags from his breathing-tank. "Well, do you think you have learned enough to fool the Vred?"

Vince shrugged. "I learned what you recorded."

"I hope so. Hiss-hiss-hiss. They are not easy to fool—many have tried, for the loot on Shann is a great attraction. Let me do as much of the talking as possible. Pretend your Lenjan is limited. You know enough Onsian to make a few remarks to me, as if seeking guidance. If they wish to hear your native language, use it—the Nesse assure me it will be unrecognized. And pretend, if you will, to be sicker than you are. That will explain a certain amount of dullness. Hiss-hiss-hiss!"

Vince couldn't help grinning. Gondal was certainly a practical being.

The four Vred who boarded were more nearly humanoid than Vince had imagined, though their quadruped ancestry showed. Their unshod feet had something of the appearance of paws. Their hands, four-fingered with no thumbs, seemed deft enough. They had good-sized heads, thick short snouts, carnivore's teeth, and medium-sized erect ears. Pelts were thick and smooth, brown with a darker tinge along the back. They wore brief single-piece zipper-garments of some woven material, quite elastic so that it fit snugly. Each had a belt and holster with some kind of handgun. Each wore a collar that, Vince decided, was communicator and recorder. The quartet was in contact with their ship, standing off somewhere with weapons trained.

The questioning was terse, mainly directed at Gondal, who was obviously a frequent guest of Shann. One of the four came and peered at Vince's eyes, then said something to the others in an odd, clipped, half-whistled language.

One important transaction took place: Vince, as he'd been advised, turned over to this boarding party all but one of the Lenj coins Leoor had given him. The things caused quite a stir, the inspectors staring and exclaiming before radioing excitedly to their ship. Now, it seemed, Vince possessed a huge credit-balance on Shann!

Finally the leader told Gondal, "Hop to within one million miles of Shann and wait instructions." The four left.

Gondal, after carefully watching the departure, turned his breathing-orifice toward Vince. "Hiss-hiss-hiss! Now your tentacles are about the enemy's torso! You will have to go through with the eye operation whether you like it or not. They are familiar with cataracts, and reported your ailment as such."

Vince swallowed. As time passed, he wasn't getting any happier about being operated upon by some alien. Still, it was better than going blind.

CHAPTER FIVE

GONDAL's huge multiple ship stayed in orbit, while Vince, Gondal, and the contingent of Gondal's crew landed in the "quaint" vessel that was supposed to be Vince's.

Vince was delighted that he didn't have to pilot the ship down. They dropped through a thunderstorm that battered as if with giant hammers, shoved them around, and threatened to turn them nose-down. If he'd had any doubt that a sunless world could have weather, he knew better now! Gondal, leg-tentacles wrapped around whatever was handy for anchorage, hissed at him cheerfully, battled the storm, and eventually brought them right-end-up into lower air less turbulent but laced with rain. It wasn't until they were down to a few thousand feet, homing on a radio beacon almost obliterated by static, that Vince saw the field lights below them.

The brightest concentration formed a hexagon at least two miles across. Within that, points of light were scattered, tending to concentrate near the edges. From each side of the hexagon, straight lines stretched away. Presently he made out the lines of buildings adjoining the hexagon—big rectangular structures like hangars.

The scattered lights, he realized, were landed ships. Here and there, lightbeams swept, some from the ships, others obviously headlights of ground vehicles.

His pulse stirred. This was a busy port!

Gondal began talking. "Those radiating straight lines are boulevards. There is much sin here. Hiss-hiss-hiss! And a reasonable amount of quieter business. And see those domes, along the brightest-lit boulevard? Those are filled with exotic atmospheres for non-oxygen-breathing patrons." Gondal activated a magni-viewer and zeroed it on a massive stone building with lesser ones around it. "There, to the east of the field. It is called east because of Shann's rotation, even though there is no sun to rise. Those are the bank buildings. The biggest one is Main Depository, where the richest loot is stored—ostensibly, at least."

"Oh." Vince studied the building for a minute, then turned to the wide-angle viewer.

The field and boulevards fit into an irregular area about ten-by-fifteen miles, with odd-shaped bites out of three sides. Vince realized those were seabeaches. They were all lighted, and seemed to be busy resorts.

The side that was not seashore was a straight line about twelve miles long, with a lighted fence along its length. On the other side of the fence was an only spottily lit area which he took to be the farmlands described by Gondal. Beyond those, he knew, the island widened and extended two-hundred-odd miles roughly parallel to the mainland coast.

Gondal was cursing softly and trying to hear radio instructions. Finally they slowed, moved laterally on gravs to the darkest side of the field, chose a spot among ships already aground, and landed. The Onsian's tentacles roved, turning off things. Shipboard noises died until there was only the hum of an air conditioner and the thrum of rain against the hull. As Shann's air began to creep in, Vince recognized a faint smell of ozone. Natural enough, in a thunderstorm.

Gondal uncoiled himself. "You will be escorted to the hospital. My part is finished except for moving this ship over to a repair facility managed by an individual named Narret. The Vred will deliver it back to you when it is repaired. Your credit-balance being what it is, you will need no money." His snakeheads hovered as his two pairs of eyes studied Vince. "The Nesse did not tell me their plans for you, but I presume plans exist."

Vince grinned. "I suppose they do. Well, thanks. Will I be seeing you again?"

Gondal hissed amusement, then got another lungful of his air. "So you do not know whether they had further chores for me! They do not. But as business will keep me here for a while, we may encounter one another again, if your treatment is not too confining. I wish you luck."

Vince suppressed another grin. He wasn't going to volunteer any information about his deal with the Nesse. "I wish you luck, too." He turned and made his way—under Shann's gravity now—to the lock.

He didn't have to climb handrails down from the lock. A small grav truck, like a jeep without wheels, hovered just outside. The driver and a guard, both armed Vred, dressed like the four who'd boarded the ship in space, sat eyeing him for a moment before the guard spoke. "You are Vinz Kul Lo?"

"Yes."

The guard reached out a four-fingered hand to help Vince into the vehicle. "We are to deliver you to the hospital of Thood Hivvis, who waits you."

The trip to the edge of the field was so short Vince had little opportunity to study the assorted alien ships parked nearby. Mostly, though, they were squat cylinders of various sizes, with widely divergent openings and protuberances—some of which were obviously weapons-ports. A few had their own integral elevators, with niches for them to fold into when not used. Some had, for ladders, simple handholds like his own.

The notable exceptions to the cylindrical shape were a trio of huge dumbbell-shaped craft, pairs of fifty-foot spheres joined by thick short "handles," each sphere resting on a set of retractable landing-legs.

There were no slim, streamlined ships like his own. He was beginning to feel a trace of embarrassment about that ship now.

As to the alien crews—seeing several different species

within a few minutes dazed him and aroused mindless, primordial fears.

There were not, as some Earthmen had imagined, any mountainous creatures, nor any tiny ones. The biggest he saw were vaguely reminiscent of Terran grizzlies, but no larger than Gondal. The smallest were the size of large collies, though they didn't look canine. There was one species that, for an instant, made him think of an ostrich or a moa. He saw only one individual hopping out of a ship's ground-level hatch. The vestigial wings had joints that flexed like shoulder and elbow, and terminated in reasonably handlike members. The feet, though, were bird-like.

His escort deposited him before a long, low building. He fought down the primitive anthropoid inside him that wanted to run to the deepest shadow and crouch there, snarling and stood still for a minute while his pulse and breathing quieted. He felt a tendency, though, to breath too hard—no doubt an effect of the extra carbon dioxide in Shann's air.

A ramp, suggesting patients in wheelchairs, ran up to a pair of flush, featureless doors in the equally flat end of the wooden building. He glanced back at the two Vred seated motionless in the grav truck, watching him, picked up his valises, and strode as casually as he could up the ramp. The doors swung open, revealing a well-lit ante-room. He stepped in, started a little as the doors closed behind him, and stood peering around. There were other doors, all closed. Various gadgets high on the walls must be sensory apparatus studying him.

A dry, whispery voice from somewhere said, "This way, please." A single door swung open. He gulped, stepped through, and found himself in a corridor that must have run the length of the building. Doors lined each side. One, a little ways along, opened noiselessly. He walked to it, stepped into a moderately small room—and went rigid.

CHAPTER SIX

THE CREATURE that crouched to one side of the narrow bed gave, at first startled glance, the impression of a monstrous, squat spider.

After a moment of shudderng, Vince controlled himself. The idea of a spider, he told himself firmly, was only his subconscious mind grasping at a simile. This creature had twelve legs, not eight; and they were obviously fleshed and boned like a warm-blooded creature's. They terminated not in claws, but in three-digited hands, each slim finger having three or four joints. No minority of those legs, he decided, could support the creature without the rest. They grew equally spaced from the rim of the body (which was shaped like a thick discus twenty inches across) and angled themselves to give support all around. Those legs, if straightened, would be about eighteen inches long. As it was, they bent so that the belly almost touched the floor. The thought flashed through Vince's mind that they could launch the creature in a spring.

But the only mouth he could see wasn't formidable. It was in a head, collie-sized, on the end of a flexible neck that sprouted from the body near one edge. There was a snout, and a pair of beady eyes, that made him think of an otter.

The neck stretched itself, making him flinch. The whispery voice came from the otter-like mouth. "Please be welcome. I am Thood Hivvis. I wanted to look at you immediately because—" the eyes blinked in a way that suggested amusement. "I must assemble certain equipment, and I was not sure of your body-shape. I see that you are not unlike the Nesse—Do you know of them?—though bulkier." The legs moved in a quick little chain-step, carrying their owner to one side. "Please make yourself comfortable. Sit on the bed, if you wish. This will be your room while you are here."

Vince, aware that he'd been half-crouching, walked to the bed and sat down. Hearing the creature speak lessened his horror of it—a little. "I, uh, thank you. You're the proprietor here?"

Thood Hivvis tilted his head a little. "Proprietor and chief surgeon. Surgery is a specialty of my race—as you can see, we are well equipped for it." Several of the legs lifted, to demonstrate. "Do not concern yourself that I have not a larger establishment. There are nurses and technicians here, and a few apprentice surgeons who perform non-critical work; and I can always call in consultants. Shann boasts a considerable medical community."

Vince sighed. "I've been told you're entirely competent. Are you familiar with my ailment? I'm no medical man myself, but I understand there's more to the treatment than an operation on the eyes."

Thood Hivvis waggled his head. "The virus needs killing, yes. A tedious process, but one for which specific medicines exist. The rest of your body will restore itself, once the virus is dead. But the eyes—that opacity of the lenses will not reverse itself. They must be removed. You are familiar with the structure of your eyes?"

"Well . . . vaguely."

The beady eyes studied him. "You are a little nervous, are you not? Please do not doubt my qualifications. I have examined and repaired the eyes of more species than I would care to list at one telling. I am the author of treatises used by medical practitioners of the most advanced races. Before my, ah, legal difficulties I was. . . . But no matter. I know optics as—Shall we say?—Gondal knows piracy."

Vince sat staring at the creature uncomfortably. He noted for the first time that it was covered with very fine dark-brown fur, and that it wore no garments except a

39

delicate collar or necklace that might include a communicator. "I'm sure you are quite qualified. It's just that I . . ."

"Your eyes, yes. I would feel no different than you. I will leave you now. There is a bath through that side door. A meal will be sent shortly—suitable protein and some vegetables. For the first few hours we will let you rest and get accustomed to the room." Thood raised and lowered his head in what must be some kind of amenity, turned, and scuttled out the door, which closed after him.

Vince, insides churning, slipped off his boots and lay back on the bed. There were openings in the ceiling that must house viewers. He supposed he'd be under surveillance.

His mind wouldn't stay off the forthcoming operation. As he understood it, the removal of cataracts—by Earth's doctors, at least—involved slicing off a wafer of the cornea, scraping out the crystalline lens that had gone opaque, and replacing the wafer. Experiments had been tried, putting in replacements of flexible plastic or whatnot, but hadn't been successful. A man, after a cataract operation, simply had to wear thick-lensed glasses. *If* he recovered his sight at all. The medics insisted, in their reassuring tones, that the operation was almost routine.

But Earth's doctors hadn't dared try to operate on Vince.

In any case, he mused glumly, you were supposed to hold your eyes perfectly still for days after the operation, so the eye could grow back together. How the hell could a man do that, even under sedation?

He shuddered as if he were suddenly cold. Could he bear to have Thood Hivvis slicing away at his eyes? Intelligent or not, the alien *looked* like a spider. Would he, perhaps, crouch on Vince's chest?

The food was like what he'd eaten on the way to Shann. The vegetables were varied in color and texture and flavor, but more or less starchy. The fruits were—well, like fruit.

He slept twice and took several showers because, despite

the comfortable temperature, he perspired a little.

It was a vast relief when one of the nurses (humanoid males with furless brown skins) brought him a beaker of slightly milky liquid and said, "Drink this, please. We feel you are ready for the operation."

Vince took a deep breath, drained the beaker, and handed it back. The stuff was mildly alkaline with a bitter tinge like quinine—and also a good percentage of alcohol that burned on the way down and felt good in his stomach. The nurse left. He lay for a minute trying not to clench his hands nor stare toward the door where Thood would enter; then, as he recalled it afterward, he was all but asleep. He was aware that the alien surgeon arrived with assistants, and directed them in setting up various apparatus, including a sort of bridge across Vince's body upon which Thood would squat; then his lethargy deepened and he had no clear thoughts. Vaguely he knew that they did something to his eyelids to hold them open. He thought, too, they somehow fixed his eyeballs so he couldn't move them even involuntarily. Then there was a long nightmare in which he felt something working at his eyes, while he squirmed and moaned. And, finally, simple, dark comfort.

It was seven or eight mealtimes since the operation. He fumbled his way back to bed from the shower, felt about the covers to determine whether the attendants had changed the sheets yet (they had), then lay down, face upward. He was getting damned sick of this room and of the bandage over his eyes. The only times he'd been out of the room were when they let him fumble his way along the corridor for exercise.

He lifted a hand and felt again of the bandage. The edges were as close-fitting as ever. It was like a growth of some kind, as much a part of his face as his skin. He'd tried prying at it with fingernails until he was convinced it wouldn't come off without the skin. He couldn't honestly say it was uncomfortable. It simply drove him half-nuts.

As for moving his eyeballs—that was a joke! He felt

of them gingerly through the bandage. They might as well have been two hard-rubber balls in place of his eyes. At times he wasn't sure they weren't.

They'll tell me sooner or later, he thought sullenly. Thood Hivvis, with his damned bland bedside manner, will say apologetically that something went wrong, and I'm blind.

Oh, the nurses insisted that his eyes were all right; that the reason he couldn't even sense light in the room or corridor was that the bandage was completely opaque; and that the muscles had been immoblized temporarily and harmlessly. He didn't believe them. What material, hardly thicker than the skin of an apple, could completely filter out the light?

Yet, he told himself over and over, he *might* be wrong. A sheet of metal foil, thinner even than the bandage, could block off all light. Weren't there plastics so loaded with black pigment that they let through absolutely no light? How about the bellows of cameras? They were thin.

But, he thought, even inside a giant camera a man ought to be able to detect *some* light.

And he'd repeat again and again to himself that maybe his eyes simply weren't as sensitive as they'd been. He could bear that. If only he could see at all; even though he needed strong light. . . .

He cursed himself for being a weakling, fumbled at the small stand near the bed, found the beaker he expected, carefully extracted it from its steadying-clamps, and drained it. Then he turned over on his side and determinedly relaxed until he slept.

"Vinz Kul Lo."

He rolled over muggily, trying to blink his eyes open as he always did when he awoke, forgetting the bandage. Then he sat up so abruptly that dizziness swept over him. He clapped a hand to his face, grunted in surprise. The bandage was gone! And his eyelids popped open and shut at his will!

A ragged laugh escaped him. So he *was* blind! Though he turned his head in every direction, straining his eyes to see, there was only blackness. He contorted furiously to his feet.

Then he gasped as faint luminosity grew in the room.

The light strengthened, or seemed to. He leaped across the room and thrust out a shaking hand to grasp the door-knob he thought he saw. It was round and firm and cool in his grasp. But the door was locked. He tugged at it a few times, then whirled to stare at the bed. It was coming into focus, and brightening.

He ran to the bed and threw himself down on it, bellowing with laughter. He could see! His eyes, unused to focusing, strained and twitched, but he could see! No matter that things seemed dark, his eyes would improve, *were* improving every second! He laughed until he was out of breath, lay almost weeping for a while, then slowly relaxed.

The room was almost normally bright now.

"Kul Lo."

He turned his head toward the intercom. "Yes! I'm awake. I can see! Thood, I can see! You—"

"What can you see?"

"Why, everything! The room and the doors, the bed, the nightstand, the speaker-grill, the scanners in the ceiling—"

"Can you see that length of black thread in the corner near the door?"

Vince lifted himself on an elbow and peered. "Certainly."

"Describe it, please."

Vince scowled at the communicator grill. "What is this—don't you believe me? It's a piece of black thread on the floor, that's all. It's—oh, about a foot long if it were straightened out, and it's curved—" he sighed with exasperation, "it forms an infinity sign."

"Can you see the cracks around the door?"

"No. I never could, when the lights were off in the

room. The door fits the jam closely, and there's a molding outside. Why all this catechism? Do you think I'm crazy, or something, and only imagining I can see?"

"No, Vinz Kul Lo. But this is an entirely new experience for me, and an incredible one. Believe me, we took pains to have no light in the corridor, and to reinforce the insulation around the door. Kul Lo, I expect you to be furious when you learn the truth. That is why you are locked in your room. That is why, also, I let you think when you first awoke without the bandage that you were blind. I wanted you to appreciate your eyesight—even though I have given you, along with it, a circumstance you will not welcome."

"What in space—"

"Hear me out, Kul Lo. I did to you what I did under a threat far more compelling than simple death. I will not pretend that the opportunity to experiment and observe is not welcome; yet had I a free choice I would never have. . . . Kul Lo, I do not know the background of your relationship with Gondal, but I presume you have no illusions about him. He is a pirate, and an extremely clever one. In this case he must have been scheming for some time; and your affliction must have fit like a miracle into his plans. Or perhaps he adapted to a sudden windfall. In any case he was prepared with the blackmail I could not, cannot, resist. And he had acquired somewhere a bit of technology, a bit of medical science, that had been to me only a fantastic rumor. He came to me with the whole thing. . . . I was stunned. He had, he told me, an eye patient of precisely the right metabolism. He handed me, literally out of the sky, items I would not have believed in had he not given me undeniable proof."

Vince uttered a growl. "Well, whatever in—"

"Wait, Kul Lo. I want you to hear it in the one telling. You have been given a fantastic gift. For it, you pay with a sort of slavery. Your eyesight—any useful vision at all —now depends upon continued treatment, for a time, that only Gondal can give. Believe me, I expended every resource to try to thwart him; but I found no way. You are his slave, Vinz Kul Lo. Unless you obey him he will withhold the treatment and you will go blind."

Vince lay rigid on the bed, staring at the small grill from which the voice came. Disbelief and rage churned within him. He raised himself trembling to a sit. His voice came choked and unfamiliar. "You're not . . . joking?"

"I wish I were! No doubt you feel like killing me. I do not blame you, but I have taken precautions against it. I find that, though I am full of shame, I still want to live."

Vince got to his feet and took a few aimless steps. Could he believe all this? He let out another growl. Yes, Gondal surely smelled something big in Vince's association with the Nesse. The damned snakehead!

A measure of calmness overtook him. "All right," he told the grill, "you're correct—I do want to kill you! As for Gondal—"

Thood's whispery voice said, "I wish you nothing but luck against him. But do not destroy your chance of keeping your eyesight. The treatments must continue for several hundred hours, and already I have used up the carefully measured supply of medicine he gave me. Clever! He's so damnably clever, and without fear. . . .".

Vince found his fists clenched and forced them to relax. "He'd better be clever! I'll live with just one purpose! For now—what's this great gift you claim to have given me?"

"You are experiencing it. Kul Lo, how much light would you say there is in your room?"

"Why . . . the usual amount. I couldn't see by it at first, but my eyes seem to be normal now. As good as they were before I got the virus!"

"Is there any trouble focusing?"

"No, not since I first woke up."

"You see all colors well?"

"Certainly. Why not?" Vince stiffened. "Oh! It didn't occur to me. I'm—I'm supposed to need thick glasses, but I don't! Did you—did you install something?"

Thood made the gurgling sound that was his laugh. "Indeed I did—that was Gondal's contribution. I am glad the focus is easy; I tried very hard to assure that. But the fantasy is in the level of illumination. The room doesn't seem dim?"

Vince swore impatiently. "I told you it didn't!"

"Can you see the, ah, strips where the luminosity usually appears?"

Vince turned to scan the room, frowning. "I can see where they are. But they don't seem . . . Why, they're not luminous at all! The light comes from the walls and ceiling!"

Thood sighed. "There is *no* light in your room, Kul Lo. No light that I nor any natural being—even the native animals of Shann, who are adapted to starlight—could detect. We went to great pains to remove any trace of phosphorescence; any instrument that might emit the faintest radioactivity. When you awoke awhile ago, the darkness was complete. Then we applied to the room a weak electromagnetic field. The light you are seeing by originates in the pigment of the paint on the walls and ceiling—a glow so feeble no instrument we possess can register it. A faint ghost of light excited by the electro-magnetic field."

Vince stared at the speaker-grill in disgust. "What are you handing me? I—I'm no optician or physicist, but I know that there's a minimum threshold of light necessary for any kind of detection, by natural organs or synthetic instruments!"

"Yet you see the glow all about you?"

"Yes, damn it; I see a glow!"

"Well, Vinz Kul Lo, the explanation is this. What I put in place of your eye-lenses were no simple wafers of plastic; they are extremely miniaturized, complex things involving their own power source—which is automatically recharged whenever you look at any light of moderate intensity—and an in-situ system of intensification. Let me make it plainer. Between the time a light ray enters the front surface of your eye and the time it emerges into the vitreous humor—a distance of less than three millimeters —it is intensified as much as two million times. But only if it is very faint to start with! Stronger light is either passed through unchanged; or, if it is very strong, partially absorbed. The result is, you can see under a tremendous range of brightnesses. When you walk forth upon the surface of Shann—away from the artificial lights, I mean—you will be able to see by starlight as clearly as you ever did by the sunlight of your native planet." Thood paused. "You will not, of course, be able to see the full range simultaneously—that would involve a ratio of perhaps trillions-to-one! Your eye will necessarily make adaptations, as it has always done." Thood sighed. "What I would not give to change places with you!"

"Well, why in hell didn't you?"

"It was impossible, even if Gondal had agreed. Not every species has a metabolism that will accept this thing. And Gondal knew what he was looking for. There is, not to mention your bodily chemistry, the matter of your physical form and your temperament. You humanoids make good pirates."

Vince barked a laugh. "Obviously, so do Onsians! By the way, if I may presume to ask, what in hell does Gondal want with a slave who can see by starlight?"

"He did not, of course, confide in me. But think, Vinz Kul Lo—here on Shann is stored loot that could ransom whole planetary systems. And Shann is a world of perpetual darkness, away from the artificial lights. Can you not guess what Gondal wants from you?"

CHAPTER SEVEN

BY THE TIME Vince saw Gondal again, he had his rage fairly well under control. The meeting took place in the control room of Vince's now-repaired ship. They were going on a short hop off Shann, ostensibly to test out the repairs. Gondal, after takeoff, made an extremely painstaking search of the vessel to make sure they weren't bugged with listening devices.

The Onsian got a lungful of his air-mixture. "You do not show the anger I expected."

Vince, keeping the murder out of his face, ran his eyes over the alien's bulk. He wondered what he could do with his fists against such a creature, if it came to that. "I'm angry enough. But I'm not inclined to commit suicide." He met first one pair, then the other, of the Onsian's eyes. "You went to a lot of trouble to assure my cooperation. Why?"

Gondal waved a tentacle impatiently. "Let us not play coy games. Thood Hivvis, who is passably honorable when permitted to be so, has undoubtedly told you as much as he could. One facet of the situation he does not comprehend, because he lacks knowledge of your background. Your being isolated, unreachably far from your own species and from your sponsors, the Nesse, makes you even more dependent upon me. I could have chosen individuals of other species upon whom the operation could have been performed. But I'm sure you can see the advantages of having, shall we say, a more helpless partner?"

Vince was silent for a minute, thinking hard. He still

wasn't sure Gondal didn't have ideas about Vince's project for the Nesse. In any case, the pirate would be alert for any opportunity. "In other words, the more helpless your slave, the less chance he'll find some way of double-crossing you. Certanly, I see that. You must lead a nervous life, not being able to trust anyone!"

"Hiss-hiss-hiss! It is, indeed, precarious at times. But exhilarating, and often profitable. And speaking of profits, you have not yet heard my proposition for you."

Vince said, "I think I have. Do as you order, and I'll keep my eyesight!"

Gondal made a disgusted gesture with two upper tentacles. "Oh, come, come! I'm no over-greedy fool, to use only threats without sweets. This is my offer: if we succeed, you shall have one-tenth the loot. Unless, of course, we incur crippling expenses—in which case we should have to arrive at some accommodation. You are indeed a naïve being, Vinz Kul Lo, as regards the normal practices of outlawry. Respectable businessmen can afford to cheat one another as opportunity arises. We successful pirates are bound by a sterner set of laws—before we create a grudge, we must consider future retaliation. Oh, underlings will often sell out an employer, if offered adequate bribes—that is an accepted part of the game— but entrepreneurs of my level keep their word. Many pirate chieftans command the firepower to blast me out of the sky, or have influences and knowledge no less deadly. No, Vinz Kul Lo, outlaws of substance do not cheat one another. You had best learn that well, since you are posing as one of us."

Vince couldn't help a short laugh. "Don't try to butter me up; I know my position. I'm one of the 'underlings' you mentioned."

Gondal's snakeheads came to rest while the two pairs of eyes stared speculatively at Vince. The Onsian got another lungful of his breathing-mixture. "I see, Vinz Kul Lo, that you do not yet grasp the enormity of what I have given you. I spoke of entrepreneurs, and indeed I have invested a great deal in this undertaking. But money is only one kind of resource. Those altered eyes of yours, innocent one, are a tremendous asset! Consider—all of space is dark except for those few trivial vicinities of stars, or where artificial lighting exists. But not dark to you! Think of the weapon you wield!"

Vince didn't bother to keep the scorn out of his reply. "And yet, you hold a club over me."

Gondal sounded genuinely hurt. "You cannot blame a person for carrying a little insurance. I have placed a mighty weapon in your hands. Am I unnatural in realizing that it might be used against me?"

Vince allowed himself a grin. "Thanks for pointing it out. Also for the implication that once you're through with me, I'll be too dangerous to be left alive. You see, I'm not *entirely* naïve. Well, all that's for the future. Let's talk about *now*. You've got me where the hair's short, and I can't refuse to cooperate at least to some extent. Specifically what do you want me to do?"

"Hiss-hiss-hiss. You show fangs! But I have seen fangs before. We cannot plan in detail yet, Vinz Kul Lo. For the present, merely familiarize yourself with Port-Of-Shann and with as much of the rest of Shann as possible, though you will find your movements restricted to this island. Learn the customs of proprietors and patrons. Observe things that only you can observe. Then, when we know more—for I too will be busy learning things—we will scheme." Gondal refilled his lungs from the back-cannister. "Now there is another matter to discuss before we return to Shann. The Nesse did not send you here out of charity. They want something done for them. Whatever it is, it will not be easy for a lone person unfamiliar with the place and with intrigue in general. Why do we not extend our partnership to include your obligation to the Nesse? It may be that I can give indispensible help."

Vince got to his feet and stretched. "I'll think about it."

Gondal sighed. "You still do not trust me. All right, keep the secret—I cannot rebuke you, on ethical grounds, at least. But it would be safer for both of us if we pooled our problems and resources. Well, we had best go back now. Has Thood Hivvis returned your passport, so that you'll be able to prove credit?"

Vince patted a pocket. "Yes." He noted the Onsian's quick look. Did Gondal suspect anything about the wallet? Or did he merely wish to study it and possibly learn something of Vince's background?

They landed. Gondal left the ship. Vince waited until he was gone, then closed all hatches, turned out all lights (including the tiny ones on the control panel), and pulled the wallet from his pocket. To his new vision, the wallet glowed with a faint purplish-blue light, a spill-over, he supposed, from the latent power stored in the thing. He went to the door and peered aft along the dark corridor. Dark—and he'd have to learn to recognize such darkness—but not *entirely* dark. To him, there was a definite diffuse glow from aft, where the fissionable fuel was stored.

He was beginning to realize that Gondal had not exaggerated the usefulness of his gift.

CHAPTER EIGHT

VINCE retreated deeper into the shadow between two hangars.

Neither of the two Onsians who were renting a shuttle-boat was Gondal, but wherever any of the pirate's crew went was of interest to Vince. Gondal himself had been missing for several hours.

The pair squirmed into the boat (a utility model with clear windows on all sides, ceiling, and deck), closed the hatch, and took off. Vince moved to where he could watch them start east. If they didn't swerve, they'd cross the farmlands and head along the landward shore of the island. Whether their purpose was innocent or not, the course would hardly interest radar monitors—it was the one prescribed for an unguided sightseeing tour of the wild island.

He looked around carefully to make sure no one saw him emerge from his spying-place, then hurried to the rental agency. A Vreddan clerk bowed as he approached. Vince extended his wallet, glancing at it with a stir of nervousness even though he couldn't see the faint glow in this lighted place. "I'm convalescing here for a while. I understand I can rent a boat and fly around the island for a look at it."

"Yes, sir." The clerk looked swiftly through the wallet, turned to punch studs on a keyboard, and watched symbols scroll across a small screen. "Certainly, Patron Kul Lo. Our smallest model should suit you if you are going alone. You will find maps and information available by video from Central Data. If you do not find what you wish in the boat's index, simply ask Central by voice. The standard map on the boat's viewer will show points of interest as well as the flyway. A moving blue dot will represent your boat, turning orange should you accidentally stray off-limits. There are well-lit bathing beaches on the leeward side of the island, safely fenced in. In general you may fly anywhere over the island, but please do not attempt to land except in fenced areas, as there are dangerous predatory beasts. Should you desire to fish at sea, you may, upon request, obtain clearance to fly seaward as much as fifty miles. The weather is quite calm just now."

Vince strove to hide his impatience. "Thanks. All I want is a brief look for now."

"Very well, sir." The clerk indicated a boat just moving to the takeoff spot.

Vince climbed in and shut the hatch. He sat for a moment studying the controls. What a dolt! Why hadn't he spent an hour or so of the time he'd fretted through since his talk with Gondal, and learned how to fly a shuttleboat? But things seemed adequately labeled. He turned on the switch marked, Main Grav Drive, found the toggle-handle with directional arrows around it, located the vertical-rise control, and took off, trying to show no nervousness. After brief experimentation he headed east across the farms.

The map the clerk had mentioned already glowed on the main view-screen, a color transparency that looked almost like a photograph. He veered slightly to center the boat in the flyway, then raised his eyes to look for the vehicle he was pursuing.

It was very strange being able to see by starlight. Though the artificial lenses installed in his eyes cut down the intensity of any bright star so that it didn't dazzle him, he was able to see so many that the total effect tended to be blinding. At least, he couldn't pick out a small object already miles ahead. He let himself stare around for a minute, taking in the splendor of the sky—which looked like photographs taken through rich-field telescopes. That dark nebula, above and to his right—did it have a familiar shape? No, of course not—he was hundreds of light-years from anything visible from Earth.

He started suddenly. That bright globular shape up there —was it a ship coming in? He grinned and relaxed. It was one of Shann's two moons, lit by starlight. Bigger than Luna but farther from its primary. He pulled attention away from it and explored the boat's radar system. It ought to show, as a precaution against collision, any other boat near enough to . . .

Yes! That must be the Onsians ahead of him. They were moving, as he was, slowly, no doubt to avoid drawing the attention of some radar monitor back at the field.

Or, he reminded himself, they might honestly be on a sightseeing tour. Even pirates might be curious about a world like Shann.

He was over the farm area now. He could see the crops clearly—fruit orchards, wide, neatly tended fields of low growing plants similar to tomatoes or sugar beets, grain fields in various stages of ripening. These must be native grains, able to use starlight. They did seem much more leafy than their Terran counterparts. There were no animal farms. The meat he'd been eating must be wild game.

He reached the eastern fence of the area. It was at least twenty feet high, of strong wire mesh, angled outward at the top and no doubt electrified. A road paralleled it just inside. To his left, not more than two miles away, was a group of buildings and some parked shuttleboats and ground vehicles. That was where the fence reached the coast. He could see a ground car just starting out on what might be a circuit of the colony's fences; and—yes, his radar showed air vehicles making the rounds too.

He crossed the fence and angled a little to his left to reach the island's leeward coastline. The boat he was following hadn't made such a turn, but he didn't want his pursuit to be obvious.

There were dozens of patrons on these up-island beaches—bipeds, quadrupeds, and a few of the less familiarly formed species that still made his skin prickle. A few were fishing. He saw one bear-like being haul in a yard-long slender catch that had at least six pair of fins, long feelers more elaborate than a catfish's, and spiny protection all over.

Farther up-island the beaches were deserted. Perhaps most guests felt nervous about the dense jungle that overhung the fences in some spots.

He glanced at the radar-map. The Onsians had moved out to the shoreline and slowed. Pulse quickening, he climbed a hundred feet and took a winding course above the surf that should bring him over the other boat. He turned out all his lights, though of course he could do nothing to hide himself from their radar.

When he found them they'd landed on a small beach —the last fenced one—and were out of the boat.

He didn't dare pause more than a few seconds. Instead, unwilling to go past, he turned inland and drifted slowly as if watching the jungle-top.

With illumination (for him) coming from the full sky, there were no deep shadows. He saw small lemur-like creatures with huge eyes, leaping from branch to branch, pausing to peer around intently. Birds, some of them with feathers, some without, flitted everywhere. Even with the hatch closed, he could hear their calls. They too had oversized eyes.

There was one big salamander-like thing that seemed to have no eyes at all. Instead, it moved very slowly, turning its head this way and that as if hunting by sound. Or maybe it used infrared sensors, like some Terran reptiles. He paused with a stir of horror to watch it find a bird's nest, put the owner to distracted flight, and curl, leisurely about the nest.

He turned back toward the beach. The Onsians, their breathing-cannisters still strapped to their backs, cavorted in the surf like weird octopi.

What now? The monitor at the field would have him on radar plot. The landed craft would be screened by jungle and intervening hills, but there might be some telltale aboard that located it. In any case, the monitor would know he was over the same spot, and might wonder why.

Unwillingly, he turned the boat up-island and moved slowly on, looking back.

And, since he was no ordinary watcher, he was able to see one of the two Onsians strike out into deeper water.

Seconds later he saw another dark form moving inward from farther out, breathing-member thrust like a snorkel above the surface!

Dangerous or not, he brought the boat to a hover. The newcomer trudged up the slope of the beach and, still mostly submerged, met the outgoing crewman. They paused to confer, then each continued on his path.

Vince saw the incoming Onsian's breathing-appendage coil and poke beneath the surface—coupling onto a cannister, no doubt. Then, as the alien resumed shoreward progress, Vince recognized Gondal.

Dangerous or not, he moved a little closer, pulse hammering. The Onsians looked so comfortable submerged. . . . Of course! They must be natural amphibians! Vince sat grinning as he watched Gondal join the crewman on the beach.

So the other crew member was going out to take Gondal's place at some secret lair in the channel! Or . . . Vince peered northward. Twenty miles away loomed the mountainous edge of the continent. Could an Onsian wade, or swim, that far? Would he dare? According to pamphlets, a considerable array of formidable sea creatures lurked in the depths.

But Gondal was not timid.

Gondal and the crewmen were in the rented shuttleboat now. Vince watched them take off and move back toward the colony. He wondered if the rental clerk would notice a substitution of individuals.

But Gondal, of course, would have timed things to take advantage of a shift-change.

Vince watched the boat out of sight, then glanced at his map. Already he was near the edge of the permitted flyway, so he didn't dare follow the Onsian still wading into the channel, but he could still see him for a while. At least, he had a fair fix on the direction.

It must have been some marginally noticed movement below him that made him look down. And, in the fringe of jungle along the narrow beach outside the fenced area, he saw movement again.

A great, grey, simian form—No, more nearly manlike! —took three or four swift strides and began to climb a treetrunk. Fifteen feet up it paused, peering seaward, obviously trying to follow the progress of the now-vanished Onsian.

Vince's heart pounded. He'd heard that there were natives on Shann with a primitive culture, but respectable intelligence. They were banned by treaty from the island. Was this a furtive member of that species? He watched the big form climb a little higher. The humanoid must be nearly eight feet tall, muscled like a human wrestler. The eyes were long and narrow, more like a Nessen's than a human's, but somehow different—yes, the pupils were oval and vertical! Perhaps in stronger light they'd narrow to slits, like a cat's. The face was not apelike; the jaw wasn't that massive, though the nose was broad and flat.

From the sides of the head a pair of slender horns curved upward. No—not horns! Vince saw one of them writhe. Tentacles, then! He made out a smaller pair, higher on the head, growing out of tousled fur. From the way they moved, he got the impression that they were hearing-organs, not feelers.

He realized that the eyes were not relatively huge, like the eyes of the birds and lemur-like things.

Gondal's crew member was completely out of sight now. The being below Vince began slowly to descend the treetrunk.

Then, a little deeper in the jungle fringe, almost hidden by foliage, Vince saw other movement.

Horrified, he stared. Some great beast was stalking the native! Vaguely feline, its eyes were bigger than Vince's fists; its cheek-whiskers like knitting needles. Its bulk must be twice that of the manlike prey.

Vince didn't know what prompted him. Possibly it was that the imperiled being had spied upon Gondal—a tenuous bond with Vince, but enough. In any case, Vince's hands moved fast. He jabbed at a stud marked Forward Searchlight. A beam, blinding for a moment, slashed out. He seized a toggle and aimed it downward, directly upon the predator.

The stalking creature threw one involuntary glance upward as it contorted in a frantic leap, huge eyes squeezing shut. Vince heard the terrified squall. Then the beast was gone into the jungle, violently shaking foliage marking its retreat.

Meanwhile, the manlike being vanished.

Vince, trembling with excitement, let the boat hover until he was sure nothing more could be seen below, then slowly put the boat into motion.

With less on his mind, the trip around the island would have been fascinating. As it was, he barely saw the rugged headlands and sheltered coves of the seaward coast, nor the flocks of bulging-eyed seabirds that dove and screamed like weirdly misshapen Terran gulls. He got back to the colony, turned in the boat, and strode around the field's perimeter to where his ship was parked.

CHAPTER NINE

GINGRANIBREN (Geegee for short, to his friends) crouched absolutely motionless and quiet in a cave-like recess between the boles of two huge, old wenniweeble trees. The trees, he mused absently, had been straining against one another, contending for the same patch of ground, long before his father's father's father was born—even before, no doubt, the coming of the Vred to Shann. Thus did lifeforms, even trees, find it incumbent to exert all their might to hold whatever niches the Die Casters saw fit to assign them.

His knife—a long, beautifully curved, highly polished blade of stainless steel obtained in swap from the Vred—was held between his hip and one of the tree-boles so that no glint of starlight might reflect from it. The eyes of a kantabeleen were sharp; and he knew the huge predator would not have retreated far despite its moment of panic when the alien flying-box suddenly turned on a light.

Geegee was very angry with himself. Not only had he become so absorbed in spying upon the strange antics of the Onsian pirate whom he knew as Gondal that he'd forgotten the more elementary caution, but, in his own startled flight, he'd left his spear leaning against the trunk of the tokonku tree he'd climbed.

He certainly hadn't acted like the son of a chief!

Very slowly, he shifted one of his ear-antennae to a new position. The normal sounds of small jungle animals going about their life-business had resumed by now, but he thought he'd better not move for a while more; even though one cog of his mind screamed at him that he must hurry back to his squad and get them off the island before the Vred arrived, alerted by the alien in the flying-box. The Vred gave very short shrift to any ipsisumoedan caught on the island. Furthermore, for the son of Chief Hakoor to be found here might bring woeful trouble to the whole tribe. Just now, when the tribe was swapping spy reports with the pirate Gondal, it would be especially bad.

However, it would do no good to hasten excessively and get himself killed by the kantabeleen—his remains would be proof enough for the Vred. And, as long as he must crouch here for a few heartbeats longer, the time had best be spent in thought.

The alien flying-box, for instance. He had not been aware of it until the sudden light thwarted the kantabeleen. But surely, hovering there without lights, the stranger must have been spying upon the Onsians. Geegee's lips curved in pleasure. This was a delightful game he was involved in—he was accepting pay (with the knowledge of the tribe, of course) from Gondal, for spying around the mainland mountain called Weeping Woman; he'd undertaken on his own to spy upon Gondal and possibly learn something of the pirate's schemes; and now this stranger had placed his hand upon the dice by spying upon Gondal. And no doubt the Vred were busy with counterspying of their own.

The stranger puzzled Geegee most of all, and he let that cog of his thinking move to the fore. He'd only caught one brief glimpse of the alien, in the spill of light from the flying-box's beam. Not a Vred, not any species Geegee knew. Was he an ally of the Vred? No way of knowing. Nor could one know whether the alien had seen Geegee. But if not, why had the alien risked discovery by turning on the light? Conceivably he was taking pictures, and wanted a picture of the kantabeleen. Geegee had seen and understood cameras, though of course he had never touched one.

Too many maybes! Optimum was to assume tentatively that the stranger, for one reason or another, might report to the Vred that he'd seen an ipsisumoedan, or some erect biped. Geegee's worry-cog stirred uncomfortably at the thought. If it were correct, Vreddan investigators would be here shortly!

He'd been here for well over a thousand heartbeats. The kantabeleen, unless it were an exceptional one, would not have waited here this long. Lithely, silently, Geegee came to his feet, knife ready. He wondered if he should strike a lucifier-torch and leave it here to divert the beast. No . . . the Vred might see the light.

Should he trot up-island to his squad and embark at once on the canoe trip back to the mainland? The risk of discovery on the water he did not spend more than a moment considering—it was a risk he ran each time he came to the island. But should he take the greater risk of going back for his spear? To lose one's spear without even being in a fight would be an ingnominious thing. But, even worse, the Vred might find the spear!

He sighed. To leave the spear there in plain sight would be unforgivable. He must take the risk of recovering it. He slipped away from the abutting trees, and, following ways his feet knew in the dark jungle, loped back toward the fenced beach. The fear-cog of his mind gibbered at him. He ignored it scornfully.

CHAPTER TEN

AFTER a few dozen hours of watching the ebb and flow of guests, it became obvious to Vince that the place to watch for Zarpi or Akorra (other than the field itself, where, of course, he'd watch for incoming ships) was along a certain one of the boulevards, where the hostelries catered especially to humanoids. He decided he'd take a room there and spend some time in various amusement places to become a known patron.

The hotel he chose was a few hundred yards from the edge of the field. It was costlier than most, with correspondingly better accommodations; but that wasn't his reason. He chose it because the grounds were dimly lighted, with many deep shadows where he could, if necessary, hide himself and watch the boulevard without being seen.

It took no more than one waking-period on the boulevard to learn that, up to now, he'd seen only a fraction of the number of humanoid or near-humanoid species that visited Shann. The place must be a stopover for all the outlaws in this cell of space!

The most numerous of any single species was a group of stocky, brown-skinned beings that, at a distance, might have been mistaken for human. Closer, their double-jointed knees and elbows and their three-digited hands would correct the error. So would one look at the broad faces with tiny eyes in folds of flesh, and wide, flat nostrils. The latter were mere boneless bulges of flesh with openings that could close tight. Vince wondered if they'd evolved on some world scourged by dust storms.

They spoke Lenjan with queer lisping voices through wide thin-lipped mouths that occasionally showed glimpses of serrated teeth. He learned via casual conversation that they were not pirates, but a contingent manning four fighting ships of a world in rebellion against an empire.

The grizzly-like beings, whom he'd seen at the field about the dumbbell-shaped ships, were interesting once he got over his awe at their size. They spoke excellent Lenjan in harsh but pliant deep voices. Their attitudes were frankly crude, with a droll cynicism that wouldn't have sounded strange in some men he'd known.

It wasn't until he learned the name of their species that he began to avoid them. They were Chullwei!

There was a rolly-polly, blue-skinned species who had manlike hands but whose heads were startlingly elongated from front to back, split by mouths that ran around the entire fronts, small round holes for ears, dual noses (one for each widely separated nostril) and wide-set amber eyes that, shockingly, could rove individually as well as coordinate for binocular vision. Ruffs of short, coarse hair ran along the middles of their shiny scalps and down their necks, how far, he couldn't see, as they all wore loose cloaks covering most of their bodies. Some wore single oculars over one eye, held on by elastic bands around the heads.

Another species was slim and graceful except that they had knees offset by a full three inches. Vince wondered how in the world—any world—they'd evolved like that. They were pale-green, hairless, and retiring. They stood about unobtrusively, big, moist eyes roving. Across their delicate features flickered expressions he took to be amusement, disgust, curiosity and, unmistakably, greed. Vince caught several of them eyeing him intently, but they all looked away as soon as they met his glance.

There were at least a dozen more species, some hard to distinguish from one another. All spoke Lenjan.

Serving all, regulating all, quickly quenching any sort of trouble, were the Vred. They were courteous but firm, unobtrusive but omnipresent. Anywhere one went, dining room, tavern, gambling-house, or show spot awhirl with exotic dances, the service was the same—the Vred would quickly have his photo on a screen and call him by name.

The field itself was no less busy.

During one half hour he watched a dozen or more big lorries trundle from the main ships' chandleries to vessels parked at various spots. Each bore some bulky item that needed heavy cranes to lift it. Most were carefully covered with tarpaulins; and in some cases, when the transfers were made to the waiting ships, grav cars hovered with curtains suspending below them to thwart prying eyes.

Smaller ground trucks delivered lighter provisions—sacks of grain, large chunks of meat in plastic, and canned goods in cartons looking very much like Earth produce except for the unfamiliar stenciled names. There were what looked like oil or gasoline drums, possibly for trade on backward worlds. He got to recognize several kinds of fissionables in heavy-gauge maroon containers of about fifteen gallons capacity. Always, when he saw those in the dark, the eerie purple-blue glow surrounded them, though only he could see it.

He was, he thought wryly, a walking Geiger counter. Except that he didn't click.

As time passed, he knew more and more of the colony's functioning. Meats, a greater variety than he'd realized, were brought in by hunting parties. Their headquarters, and the meat-processing buildings, were a quarter of the way around the field from the ships' chandleries. A steady stream of shuttleboats came and went like ants. Most were a model seating four Vred huntsmen with van space behind for ten or more sheep-sized carcasses. A few were rigged for fishing, with bombbay-like compartments underneath from which nets were dropped. The hunting and fishing, apparently, all took place on the mainland (possibly, he thought, to preserve the island's fauna for viewing by patrons). Not all the hunts were successful; more than once he saw shuttleboats return empty. But successful or not, the hunters kept regular shifts.

He also spent time watching the depositories, which, he came to understand, were pawnshops and purchasers of loot, as well as banks.

The biggest building was where the most precious items were received. Almost the size of a football field, it presented to the avenue fronting it two massive doors, thoroughly guarded at all times. If there were other openings, even for ventilation, they must be on the roof where he couldn't see them.

During one hour that he watched, four alien ships, two of them together and of identical design, landed to unload cargoes that went at once into the building. He saw the whole process of transfer; he was standing within fifty feet when the big flatbedded lorries rumbled through the briefly opened doorway, but got no hint of what the cargo was.

Within that hour at least a dozen other consignments of various sizes went into the building. One item was surprising: a truckload of baled furs, black with streaks of silver. Another load consisted of metal crates, heavily padlocked, that clinked when they were hoisted. Yet another shipment seemed to be scientific instruments of some kind.

Presently, amazed at the volume of goods that went in with very little coming out, he recalled Gondal's hint that this building might only be a front. The main vaults must be somewhere else on Shann—either that, or the whole island was hollow!

How, then, was the stuff transferred? Was there a tunnel to somewhere? Did Gondal's furtive activity in the channel relate to that? A tunnel clear to the mainland would have to be more than twenty miles long. An underwater cache in the channel? Not very plausible.

Was there any traffic on and off the island that might secretly carry the stuff?

Staring at the huge building, he suddenly grunted to himself. There *was* one regular traffic—the hunting parties!

Resisting the urge to hurry, he turned and strolled along the edge of the field, paused in deep shadow, and allowed his eyes to adjust. Now he could watch the steady stream of foragers. The boats rose from their headquarters building (apparently from an opening in the roof) and lined toward the mainland, going almost due north.

Were those boats big enough to carry the heaviest items he'd seen going into the building? No—but how many such items had he seen? Very few, actually. The boats could haul 95 percent of the stuff.

He emerged cautiously from shadow and walked out onto the field toward his own ship. It might not be the proudest vessel on Shann, might be a joke to the aliens who paused to eye it, but it had one virtue he hadn't thought of. It was tall! And, from its control room, he could get the elevated view he wanted.

A half-hour later he had an idea just where the tunnel might run. If he were planning it, he'd have it slant down from the depository, heading at first away from the field, until it was far enough out and deep enough so that simple listening-apparatus couldn't detect it. Then he'd curve it and approach the meat-processing area from the rear. It wouldn't take much of a detour. It would have to pass under a boulevard, but that was one that had no hotels—only warehouses controlled by the Vred.

All right, the theory was plausible. Where did that leave him? No doubt Gondal had already arrived at the same theory, or a better one. It still wasn't clear what specific tasks the Onsian wanted of him. Meanwhile . . .

He'd been sitting there pondering for an hour when one of his ship's instruments, which he had left on standby so it would record the comings and goings of other ships, suddenly pinged. Absently, he reached to turn on an upward-aimed viewer.

A few minutes later he writhed hastily from the seat and stood tensely before the viewer. The ships descending—four of them—were of Nessen design!

CHAPTER ELEVEN

VINCE shifted position to uncramp his legs, then wedged himself back between a girder and the outer skin of his ship. He'd crawled here by a tortuous route so he could look directly out a small ventilator-port. The view-screens of his ship could intensify any image they could pick up, but compared to his eyes they were hopelessly insensitive.

Already, he'd seen enough in open hatches of the newly arrived ships to know that armed Nesse lurked in the darkness, keeping a painstaking watch of the ships parked nearby. When an alien passed, eyeing the ships casually, the Nessen guards tensed, and one of them spoke something into his collar microphone. The alien wandered on, and the furtive guards relaxed.

Presently one of the lurking Nesse came, as if casually, into the light, leaned out the open hatch, and looked about. His long eyes turned to Vince's ship and paused. Vince felt that the alien's gaze was directly on him, but of course he was safely back from the small ventilator, in the darkness.

He noted the studious way the Nessen observed every feature of his ship.

Time passed. Then, from the direction of the Vreddan depository, a small shuttleboat approached. To his disappointment, it didn't come to one of the Nessen ships closest to him, but to a farther one, whose hatch he couldn't see. He waited. Not more than ten minutes passed, then the boat was moving away again. A searchlight followed it for a little way, then it was in relative darkness —and Vince went tense.

From the small, slowly drifting boat came a distinct purple-blue glow!

He blinked, wondering if his rudely altered eyes were playing tricks. But no, he was sure. There hadn't been any glow when the boat arrived. The natural guess was that it had picked up something from the Nessen ship with an appreciable energy-spill.

He twisted himself to peer sideways through the ventilator, watched the boat reach the big depository building and vanish into the welcoming doors. He waited a few minutes more, saw no further significant movement about the Nessen ships, and painfully unkinked himself from where he was wedged.

He crawled toward the access-door through which he'd come. But while he was still in the darkness of the space between bulkheads, he stopped, pulled from his pocket the wallet Leoor had provided him, and stood staring at it thoughtfully. The glow, insofar as he could tell, was the identical color he'd just seen coming from the small shuttleboat.

Leoor had said the wallet involved a bit of technology just recovered. Zarpi, having been able to kidnap one of the most prominent Nessen scientists, might also have managed to learn this secret!

The wallet was a Communications device. When its strange energy, undetectable in the ordinary electromagnetic spectrum, was unleashed, Leoor would be able to "hear" it at some distant watch-post. What of the similar, though much stronger, glow Vince had just seen leaving one of Zarpi's ships? Was it, too, a communicator of some kind? Or—a spy device? A means of pinpointing the secret Vreddan cache?

Hands shaking a little, he returned the wallet to his pocket. Leoor and his government suspected that Zarpi was after some stupendous Lenjan secret. Maybe Zarpi was only after the same thing Gondal was!

Of course, maybe Zarpi *hadn't* planted a spy device. It might merely be a supply of the strange fuel. Or could it be, conceivably, some kind of bomb to blast open the cache? It was hard to imagine much of the loot surviving such a blast.

He went on to the ship's control room, set the external viewers to record whatever went on around Zarpi's four vessels, then left to go back to his hotel.

With the room as nearly dark as drawn shades could make it, Vince sat on the edge of the bed, holding the wallet in his hands. He felt reluctant to use it.

Leoor had told him not to send the message that he was alive and healthy on Shann until he was definitely cured. He'd been putting that off because he wasn't sure yet—the time since his operation was too short. Now he faced the question more squarely. *Was* he cured so long as his continued eyesight depended upon Gondal? Suppose he pulled the photograph from its seat, turned it ninety degrees, closed the wallet and sat on it. The Nesse, if they got the pre-programmed message, would have no way of guessing at his difficulty. Or, if he placed the photo to send the message, "Zarpi here," without first sending the one about his health, they'd assume he was *not* healthy.

Another suggestion was that Gondal might be conscripted to help send a message-drone without the Vred knowing it. That certainly wasn't practical now! Gondal would edit any such message, or at least learn from it things Vince didn't want to reveal.

He got to his feet and took a few aimless steps about the room. He owed it to the Nesse to let them know that he was at least still able to operate. But there was no way he could do that and still hint at his difficulties with Gondal.

What it came down to was that he was entirely on his own.

He growled softly to himself. Well, so be it! He was under obligation to the Nesse, and he'd continue the best he could. After all, he didn't know Leoor's plans—conceivably they might already have Shann cordoned about, or be ready to move in quickly. He had to adhere to instructions as nearly as he could.

He opened the wallet, tugged the photo of himself free, turned it ninety degrees clockwise, replaced it, closed the wallet, and put it on the seat of the room's only chair. Feeling foolish, he sat on it. "Like a damned hen on eggs," he muttered. How long was he supposed to sit there?

He gave it about five minutes. If there were any longer time required, Leoor should have, and probably would have, so specified.

Vince repeated the process to send the message, "Zarpi here."

Finally he returned the picture to its original position, put the wallet in his pocket, and left the room. He supposed he might as well circulate among the casinos and see if he could make contact with, or at least observe, any of Zarpi's crew.

A dozen of the Nesse, he found, had taken rooms at a hotel seven or eight buildings nearer the field than his own. He'd visited the casino there once before, so didn't feel the Vred would be suspicious if he lingered now.

Presently he edged into the crowd around a table where one of the light-furred newcomers was gambling at something fairly like dice. The cubes were not numbered one-through-six, but had only five numbers plus one solid dot of silvery metal, which counted only when two or more showed face-up. There were three of the cubes, not two. Vince had already realized, without trying to work them all out, the large number of ways to make a given total. Now, he watched long enough to learn that two of the silvery dots face-up entitled the player to an extra throw, while three counted as making his point.

One of the Nesse, a quite ordinary looking individual so far as Vince could see, rolled the cubes. A deuce, a four, and a silver dot turned up. "Six," the Vreddan croupier said, and deftly punched a stud on a keyboard (which, Vince knew, would make a deduction from the player's credit-balance at Central Data).

The Nesse looked glum. "What's my balance now?"

The Vreddan touched another key and glanced at figures on a screen. "Four thousand *durs*, sir."

The Nesse gestured to his comrades. "I can't afford to lose any more. Do any of you want the cubes?"

While the light-furred aliens hesitated, Vince pushed forward. "I'd like to try my hand." He showed the croupier his identification.

The Vreddan glanced at him, punched for information, blinked, and looked at Vince again. "Certainly, Patron Kul Lo." He gathered in the cubes and extended them on a blue-lacquered paddle.

Vince took the cubes and held them in his left hand while, with his right, he reached for an inside pocket of his zipperalls. He drew out the Lenj coin he'd retained and slid it casually across the table to the Croupier. "How much is this worth? I forget."

There were no gasps, this was too sophisticated a crowd for that. However, there were a few soft alien grunts and murmurs, then an intent silence.

The Vreddan stared at the coin for a second, then slowly looked up at Vince. He drew in a breath. "Your balance is ample, Patron, unless you intend to bet very heavily. The house limits—"

Vince shrugged. "I'm thinking of buying a new ship, and want to leave my balance high. Can you give me, say, chips in the amount of fifty thousand *durs* and credit the rest to my account?"

The croupier breathed deeply again. "Certainly, Patron Kul Lo. Forgive my startlement. One does not see these objects often!"

Vince shrugged in a way he hoped would express the idea that he had more of the coins. He accepted the stack of bronze-colored plastic chips, then rolled the three cubes.

He didn't know the game, and he wasn't paying much attention, so he lost the chips rather quickly. Not, though, until after some ups and downs that kept the crowd watching—and, he had to admit to himself, excited him more than a little. Then he sighed and turned away. "Not my game, I guess."

He was careful not to glance at any of the Nesse. It had been crude enough, bringing the Lenj coin to their attention in the way he had.

CHAPTER TWELVE

Two of Vince's sleep-periods later, Zarpi contacted him.

He was in the casino of his own hotel, idly and rest-lessly gambling small sums on the dice-like game, when a voice spoke from just behind him. "Pardon me, but I have not encountered your species before. You appear very much like ourselves, except that you have little body-hair."

Vince turned, feigning casualness. "How do you do? You're Nessen, aren't you?"

"That is what we are called. Our original world was Ness."

Vince made a little bow of the head and shoulders, a common enough gesture. "The original home of my race was Carca, so we are called Carcans. Our region is far to one edge of the cell, beyond Onsi. Do you know that region?"

The Nessen said with a touch of apology, "I have never been as far as Onsi. Excuse my approaching you like this, but I was in another casino some hours ago when you mentioned the possibility that you might be buying a ship of some kind. My party has four ships at present, but we are shorthanded and might consider selling one ship. Would you care to visit us and talk with our captain?"

Vince allowed himself to look more directly at the pale-furred alien. "Why . . . my plans are not definite yet; I am still convalescing from a disease which may still linger for a while. But I suppose we might talk. Are you formal representatives of your government?"

The stranger blinked the Nessen smile. Vince's question, of course, was hardly to be taken literally here; it was a delicate way of hinting at other things. "We are hardly formal representatives of our government nor of any other. My chief's name is Zarpi. You have heard of him?"

Vince said, in the proper apologetic tone, "I have not been in this part of the cell very long."

The Nessen smiled again. "Be assured we are not snatch-and-run amateurs. The ship we offer for sale has been in our hands for a discreet period of time, and its former owners are legitimate and were properly paid. Will you visit us?"

Vince said, "I shall be greatly honored."

Vince was not, of course, encouraged to wander about Zarpi's flagship, but as he boarded he was able to see a few things. She had, he guessed, been (like the other three) a medium-sized freighter. From the outside, sealed up for space, she'd still look the part. But certain hatches concealed missile-launchers and energy-beamers and rupters (the latter being bulky weapons that beamed artificial gravity in an on-and-off sequence, variable and adjustable, that could quickly shake to bits even the sturdiest of hulls or buildings). There were armored shuttleboats, too, possibly for boarding prizes.

Zarpi awaited him in a comfortably furnished plain room.

The pirate leader was as muscular a Nesse as Vince had yet seen (though that muscularity still was of the lean, tendony sort and not bulky). One side of Zarpi's face bore a large scar (probably from an old burn) that held it partly immobile and showed thickened, darkened skin without hair.

Zarpi was intent, unsmiling, and terse of speech. "I will not maneuver about. Recently several of my men saw you cash a Lenj coin at a casino. If you have more of them, I wish to buy or trade. A ship, or something else. Lenj coins, as you no doubt understand, have a universal negotiability not matched by any single currency or coin. They would be useful to me."

Vince acted hesitant. "Well, I don't know . . . I may

have the same sort of need, in the future. You see. . . .
Well, I recently contracted a disease that threatened to
blind me quickly and kill me before long. I, uh, lost most
of my connections, and in coming here I've gotten a little
out of touch with things. Until I'm sure about my complete
recovery—which seems, now, to be likely—I can't really
plan. The only ship I own now is that ancient streamlined
job parked seventy or eighty yards away. Obviously I'll
need something else, it . . ."

Zarpi said coolly, "I hope your recovery becomes complete. Have you more of the Lenj coins?"

Vince said, "There are more on deposit here, of which
I can still claim seven, I think. I wouldn't want to part
with all of them."

The pale-furred humanoid stared into his eyes expres-
sionlessly. "That is understandable. For five of those
coins I will sell you one of these ships, fully armed and
fueled. In addition I will transfer credit here on Shann
equal to half the fair value of the ship." He watched
Vince for a moment. Then for the first time his face
showed a touch of amusement. "Even further, I will buy
your present ship at whatever the Vred will estimate as a
fair price. I can conceive ways I might use such a primi-
tive-looking ship—for instance, as bait, or for discreet
reconnoitering."

Vince sat frowning for a minute. "I guess all that
sounds pretty fair." He looked up. "I wonder, though—
as I've explained, I'm at loose ends just now, and without
connections. Would you consider, uh, taking in an associate? I could—well, I know regions of the cell that even
the Onsians don't. There are certain wealthy but militar-
ily weak worlds and empires there. I could . . ."

Zarpi said smoothly, "My obligations for the next several thousand hours would preclude such things. After
that, perhaps, if you are still at loose ends. . . . How about
the transactions I proposed? Will you make them?"

Vince sagged inside with disappointment. All he could
do now was stall, but it mustn't be too obvious. "I, uh,
think I will. But before I decide I'd like to see my physi-

cian here just once more. Can I delay for a few hours? I'll make this commitment—in any case, I'll be glad to sell you three of the coins, for a credit transfer or whatever else we can agree upon."

For just an instant, Zarpi showed annoyance. Then he made a gracious gesture. "That is reasonable. A few hours, then."

It was one sleep-period later that Vince, again visiting his ship to examine whatever his cameras might have recorded, suddenly smelled ammonia. Anger washing through him, he halted outside the control room door; then, making his face expressionless, he stepped across the sill.

The lights were off, but enough illumination bounced in via indirect paths so that he could see Gondal slumped casually against a bulkhead. "How the devil did you get in here?"

The Onsian poked his breathing-appendage toward Vince. "Hiss-hiss-hiss. I see your dark vision is as good as we hoped. May I turn on some lights?"

"Please do," Vince said woodenly. "I would not think of keeping a guest uncomfortable." He watched a tentacle reach toward the control console, feel about delicately, and locate a switch. He blinked in the sudden flood of light. "Well, what do you want?"

Gondal gestured. "Why, to inquire after your health, first of all. And then to discuss with you certain things. But, answering your first question: naturally I arranged, while I had the opportunity, that I should be able to enter this ship at will. And now, I suggest you run through your recorded scenery. There is a brief sequence that should interest you as it did me."

Vince did nothing to hide a scowl. "So you've been snooping. I hope you enjoyed the views of the field—including yourself waddling toward this ship."

"Hiss-hiss-hiss. I came in a shuttleboat, to avoid prying eyes. I suggest you examine the recordings."

Vince sauntered deliberately to the console, resisting an

impulse to kick at a leg-tentacle as he passed. "Do you mind if I darken down a bit, so I can see them?"

"By all means do so. I would not think of keeping a host uncomfortable. Hiss-hiss-hiss."

Vince dimmed the lights, activated the visual playback, and watched a view, uneventful at first, of Zarpi's ships. Suddenly he went tense.

Three Nesse appeared in a hatch and stood looking out. The two on either side seemed to be guarding, and actually half-supporting, the one in the middle.

That middle one was female.

Vince wasn't familiar enough yet with Nesse to recognize individuals surely. But he had little doubt the female was Akorra. She looked about the right age, thirty, more or less, on a human scale, and about the right size and slenderness.

She acted dull and disinterested, moving her head slowly to peer about the field. For a moment the trio stood there. Then one of the escorts said something, and he and his partner got the unresisting female turned around and they disappeared inside the ship.

Vince, realizing suddenly that Gondal's remarks about the sequence were significant, reached up and turned off the viewer. He left the light dim and faced about toward the Onsian. "So? A female, apparently ill. Maybe they brought her here for treatment."

"Hiss-hiss-hiss. You were careless, Vinz Kul Lo. You should have arranged, for camouflage, a recorded scan of the whole field instead of merely directing it at Zarpi's ships. Also, of course, I am informed that you visited one of them a few hours ago. Neither has it evaded my notice that you cashed in the last of your Lenj coins at a casino where several of Zarpi's crew were watching. Now then, I know that your credit-balance from the original deposit is ample. A rather simple speculation, is it not, that you deliberately showed the coin so Zarpi would hear of it?"

Vince felt angry dismay. "I didn't see any of you octopi around!"

"Octopi? I do not know the word, but you deliver it

like a useful imprecation. You must explain it to me some time. Hiss-hiss-hiss. I hire humanoid spies as a matter of elementary tactics. What is your interest in Zarpi?"

Vince hesitated sullenly. He had to offer a convincing lie. "Did you think I wouldn't try to make any arrangements to escape you? Zarpi is willing to sell me one of his ships. Also, I had—have—other hopes."

Gondal sighed. "The arrangement I made does not, I believe, have any loopholes. You still depend upon me for your eyesight."

"So you say."

"Hiss. I hope you will not test the truth of it! I like you, Vinz Kul Lo, and you are a costly investment. I should not care to lose you. Let us be logical in the matter of Zarpi. I think he is connected closely with your usefulness to the Nessen government. A reasonable thing, and one with which I should very much like to help you, for frankly selfish reasons. I want to maintain good relations with the Nesse. Why do you not confide in me and accept my help? It might be considerable—even indispensible. Who is the drugged female? No common tart, no associate of pirates, I am sure."

Vince felt a sinking sensation inside. He tried to stall. "Drugged?"

Gondal's tentacle-gesture was impatient. "Please, do not play games! Must I put every word in your mouth? I know already—and this should convince you of the extent of my spy arrangements—that a female Nessen scientist, one answering closely enough to the description of this drugged female, was recently kidnapped. Her field was archeology. Her specialty was Lenjan artifacts; and I know, though you may not, that she is also a physicist of great competence. Add to that your eagerness to let Zarpi know you possess some Lenj coins and a picture begins to form!"

Vince stood silent for a minute. He was glad the lights were dim. He sighed. "All right, I was careless. My job for the Nesse does involve Zarpi and Akorra." He paused.

"It was even suggested that, in certain circumstances, I might try to enlist your help. Naturally—after what you've done to me—I was, I am, unwilling about that."

Gondal squirmed his bulk into a more comfortable position. "Now we are being franker and more logical! Specifically what help were you to seek from me?"

Vince's mind raced. "Well . . . simply a matter of communications. They thought you might be able to get a message-drone and help me send it without the knowledge of the Vred here."

"Hiss-hiss-hiss. And no doubt they, and you, hoped it would not be necessary to divulge the message to me?"

Vince realized he had one hole card—the Onsian pirate didn't know he'd already sent messages, could hardly guess that there *was* any way he might contact the Nesse. "There, my many-legged friend, you are being too devious! The message was to be simple enough: 'Search is fruitful.' There was no reason to keep that from you."

Gondal coiled his breathing-appendage, connected it to the cannister on his back, and inhaled thoughtfully. Finally he uncoupled and spoke. "I can conceive reasons why that message might be kept from me, but of course, now that I know the meaning of it, they no longer apply, eh? So the Nesse hope to catch Zarpi and rescue the female. That implies certain things, does it not? Either they hope to keep track of him when he leaves here, or they plan actually to cordon Shann about and seize him, on or off the ground. Now, the practicalities of navigation and of the FTL drive place limits upon them and upon him—they taught you that much, no doubt. He cannot enter FTL closer than a certain distance off Shann, nor can he travel any significant distance without entering it. They, on the other hand, could not emerge within radar-distance and wait. So, a cordoning operation would be complex and demand large fleets. I think, Vinz Kul Lo, that your aim was to *join* Zarpi and go along with him as a spy."

Vince sighed again. "You're so damned devious that nothing underhanded escapes you! Yes, I hoped to join

Zarpi. So far he shows no interest. The Lenj coins were merely bait. Now maybe you'll be satisfied! Can you, and will you, help me send a message-drone?"

"Hiss-hiss-hiss! I would hardly decline a hand in such a delicious game, even did I not smell possible booty. But I am not naïve enough to let you send uninspected messages. I can arrange things. But you must give me the messages, and their destination; nor will you know what arrangements I make."

Vince let outward signs of anger show, but inwardly he felt a mild triumph. He'd fooled Gondal about one thing: the fact that the Nesse were already notified of Zarpi's presence. And there might be some way to fool him further, even to sneak past him a message with a significance he couldn't catch.

The surgeon, Thood Hivvis, had suggested that Vince return for a checkup every hundred hours. The first visit had been routine; the many limbed alien said that there was no sign of anything wrong and that Vince had every prospect of keeping his eyesight so long as he got the injections that only Gondal could administer. The first of those wouldn't be necessary for fifty or sixty hours yet. Vince didn't look forward to it with anything like willingness. Through his mind drifted vague ideas of overpowering the big Onsian, wresting from him whatever medicine was involved. He supposed gloomily, though, that Gondal would take adequate precautions against that.

The second visit to Thood Hivvis wasn't due yet, but for the benefit of whatever watch Zarpi might be keeping on him, Vince went early. The spiderlike alien met him blandly. "From your appearance, Vinz Kul Lo, I doubt that we'll find anything. The hormones I injected are not yet washed out of your system, and are still active. That is to say, the absence of new symptoms is favorable. However, let us check the eyes."

Thood found nothing wrong. He again sighed his wonder at the dark-vision, expressed envy, and, at the last, apologized once more for the wrong he'd been compelled (he maintained) to commit. Vince left full of frustration and dull anger.

And now, having made the visit, and presuming that Zarpi would know of it, he had no option but to see the Nessen pirate again.

He was admitted with neither eagerness nor hesitation. He sat in the same simple room, uncomfortable under the alien's cool stare. "It appears my health is good, for the moment—but some time must elapse before I can be sure of permanence. I promised to sell you three of my Lenj coins. I'll do that now, if you still want them."

Zarpi showed no emotion. "As I told you, I'll find them useful in future transactions, but not here on Shann, where there is no problem of exchange. Have you reclaimed the coins?"

"No, they're still on deposit. I can get them in an hour or so, I think. Do you know the smaller building to the left of the main depository—the Credit Center? I'll go there with you, or meet you there whenever you like. The Vred will handle the transaction after we establish our identities."

Zarpi looked scornfully amused. "I am familiar with the services of Shann. I see no reason why we can't go there now. Perhaps there will be no wait of an hour, as you suggest—the coins shouldn't be far away."

The last remark was tossed off just a little too casually —which Vince didn't miss. The thought flashed through his mind that the pirate was fishing for whatever scrap of knowledge or rumor he might possess. And, upon the heels of that thought, an inspiration trod. If he led Zarpi to suspect that he might actually know something about the Vred's secret cache. . . . "I doubt that. Being as valuable as they are, they were no doubt taken over yonder for maximum safety." He moved his head in what, if he recalled his bearings correctly, was the direction of the mainland.

Zarpi didn't quite succeed in hiding his startlement.

"Possibly so. In any case, we can make the transaction, and the Vred will deliver the coins to me later. You do not care to buy a ship?"

"Not at this time. There's still the small doubt of my future health. Besides—" Vince broke off as if he'd said too much.

Zarpi reached up to press a stud on his collar radio, and ordered a shuttleboat. They went to an outer hatch to await it. Before it arrived, Zarpi said, "Perhaps we can see more of each other, having done business together. Our species are very much alike, I think, which is always a favorable thing. Even though, as I said, my immediate future is committed, there is still the less immediate one." He made a small joke, blinking a smile, "At least, so persons like ourselves hope, eh?"

Vince smiled in return—the first time, presumably, that Zarpi had ever seen a human smile, so that it didn't have to pass the most expert scrutiny. "Indeed. And if my own future is reasonably long, there are several projects I had in mind, indefinitely delayed by my illness."

They reached the Credit Center, disembarked, entered, and found a Vreddan clerk to handle the transaction. The clerk had them stand before a scanner, palmprinted both of them, recorded their voices, and took, with a tiny instrument, minute samples of their skin and blood. Then he bowed. "The transaction is complete, Patrons Zarpi and Kul Lo." He bowed again to Zarpi. "The coins will be delivered to you, sir."

Zarpi, perceptibly absentminded, turned to Vince and offered the doublehanded grip of the Nesse. "We are friends, then, and possible future associates! Shall we take a meal together sometime soon? Not the next one, I'm afraid—I have pressing business. May I contact you?"

Vince, grinning inwardly, said, "By all means. My ship has modern communications installed, so you can reach me on the standard channel."

Vince took his departure, exulting mildly. He might have made the desired connection after all!

But that created another problem. Having hinted, as though unintentionally, that he knew about the Vreddan secret cache, it was now necessary for him actually to learn or guess something concrete so he could deliver.

CHAPTER THIRTEEN

THE VREDDAN clerk at the shuttleboat rental agency took a little longer than before to scrutinize Vince, comparing him, obviously, with the data and photos that appeared on the clerk's view-screen. "You say you want to fish, Patron Kul Lo? We have shuttleboats ready-equipped and fitted for that. Do you wish a guide?"

"No," Vince said, trying to sound casual. "A guide takes away the feeling of adventure. Just a small boat and whatever gear I'll need."

"Certainly, sir. May I suggest a few fenced coves along the seaward coast? There are several unoccupied just now, where the surf isn't too strong and the fishing is good."

Vince thought fast. "Well . . . perhaps. But I saw a party take interesting fish on throw lines not long ago, on one of the beaches along the channel side. Slender fish, with several fins. Would it be permissible to fish there now?"

The clerk hesitated briefly. "Certainly, sir. But on the channel side you're restricted to staying ashore. To seaward you can troll or drop a line into deeper water."

Vince said, "Well, perhaps I'll try that too. But I would like to have a go at the throw-line fishing on the channel side. The surf there was very mild and there was little wind. May I try that first? If I decide to do any trolling, I'll fly across the island to one of the coves you mention. That will be all right, won't it, if I report in by radio?"

The clerk bowed. "Quite, Patron." He pressed a stud to call a boat. "Before you land on the channel side, please scan the beach from aloft and make sure it isn't occupied. We'll direct any later patrons elsewhere so you won't be bothered."

"I'll do that." Vince glanced at the shuttleboat settling just outside the office door. "You say everything's already aboard?"

"Everything, including bait. And lunches you'll find palatable. The records show you rented a boat once before. You recall the programmed maps and the other routine?"

"I remember them." Vince bowed his thanks, walked to the boat, climbed in, and took off.

This time there seemed to be more ground vehicles patrolling along the fence around the farm area. He moved on, crossing the dark jungle diagonally to the channel beaches. He flew over them, staying high enough so he had line-of-sight to the field, pausing now and then as if inspecting some particular beach.

When he came to the small beach where he'd spied upon Gondal and the pirate's two crew members (and where he'd distracted the huge carnivore stalking the furry humanoid) he was dismayed to find a party of Chullwei, six or seven of them, already fishing. He didn't slow, but moved on. Now what?

The next beach down, as he recalled, was a mile farther. Could he operate from there?

It was empty. He hovered aloft for a minute, giving the radar monitors time to see that he was stopped, then lowered his boat to the sand.

Before getting out he sat studying the control board again. A light that had indicated a radar-scan upon him when he was aloft, was out now. Intervening trees and hills would surely hide him from radar. But were there other, secret devices in the boat to keep it pinpointed? Were there, perhaps, even sensors hidden about the beach, to make sure a boat stayed where it landed?

Slowly, tense with anxiety, he got together lines, hooks, and sinkers; assembled and coiled about fifty yards of throwline, baited the hooks, and climbed from the boat.

If he could make a raft of some kind, or even find a log not too heavy to propel through the water. . . . He certainly didn't want to swim! Aside from the risk of sea carnivores, it might be a long way to wherever Gondal had been.

He made one toss out beyond the surf, taking the opportunity to look unobtrusively about, though any instruments would be well camouflaged.

It was lucky that he went through the motions of fishing, for a few minutes later a shuttleboat, lightless and carrying four Vred, drifted by a few hundred yards offshore, low over the water.

He forced himself to go on casually with his fishing. He pulled the line in, found one of the long, many-finned fish on a hook, removed it and put it in the plastic cage supplied as a creel. With a length of cord, he tied the cage to the metal fence where it ran out into the surf, pushed it out so that it was half-immersed, and went back to rebait his hooks.

It was hard to act casual, with the Vreddan patrol craft hovering just offshore, its occupants watching him intently. And eerie, knowing that they thought themselves invisible while he could see them so plainly! There was little doubt that the clerk who'd rented him the boat had been suspicious enough to alert the colony's security forces. Why? Were other things going on to alert the Vred? And did it end his plans abruptly?

Unhappily, breathing a little raggedly because of the adrenalin in his blood, he pulled in the line again, found it empty, rebaited, and tossed it out again. If they were going to stay there as long as he did . . .

But then they moved on. He could see from their actions, no longer glancing at him, that they were satisfied.

Or perhaps they were just pretending. Would there be another guard boat along soon?

He took an especially deep breath and exhaled. If he were ever going to make a break, it had best be now. He hastily pulled in the line, coiled it, and tossed it in the back of the shuttleboat. Then he went to the creel cage, untied it, dumped the still-live fish back into the surf, and carried the cage to the boat. He got in, turned on power, and sat for a minute scanning the sea and sky for any other craft that might be within sight. He saw none. Leaving all lights off (except the small panel-lights he couldn't control, which worried him) he lifted just free of the beach and moved out slowly over the water.

The radar-scan light remained off. Naturally—he was still hidden from Central Monitoring. But what about the guard boat that had stopped to watch him? It would surely have its own radar. Had it gone far enough so he wouldn't show, this close to the water? He stared anxiously eastward.

The security craft had either rounded some bulge of the island, or it was too far away to see.

He accelerated, staying just high enough so an occasional wave slapped against the bottom, and moved out over the channel by dead reckoning. Gondal had slanted up-island rather than going straight out, so Vince should sooner or later cross the Onsian's course.

A few hundred yards offshore he paused to look around him. There were several boats in sight over the beaches, and others aground on them, but he saw nothing that looked official except one unlighted four-place craft that moved along above the surf, doubtless patroling. He sat watching it nervously until it was well up-island.

He was already beginning to feel like an idiot. All he had to go on was his recollection of the way Gondal had headed. There was no way of being sure the Onsian hadn't changed course before climbing into sight. And what was he looking for anyway? For all he knew, Gondal might merely have hidden some small object on the bottom of the channel. He might have equipment there, but camouflaged. And for such a vague search Vince was jeopardizing not only his aims and his liberty, but quite possibly his life! He grunted to himself in disgust. Well, impulsiveness had always been his weakness, and obviously he wasn't any smarter now. But as long as he'd embarked on this fool's chase, he'd see it through.

The channel seemed nowhere to be more than thirty feet deep or so, and the water being clear, Vince could see down through it easily. It was well that he could, for what he found wasn't obvious.

He was possibly five miles off the island, cruising low over the water on a grid-search-pattern. Now and then he glanced uneasily southwestward, where a distinct glow marked the colony's field. Central Monitoring certainly had line-of-sight to him now—the radar-scan telltale light was on—but, with luck, they wouldn't see the small blip representing him against the background of the water and, farther away, of the mainland coast. With a great deal of luck, he amended to himself, and let the shuttle-boat settle another few inches until he was almost floating.

The thing on the bottom, seen slantingly to one side, would not have caught his eye except for the triangular pattern it formed.

Heart suddenly thumping, he turned his boat that way. He shot looks in all directions to make sure nothing, such as an official boat, was approaching. Then he was over the spot and peering down.

He had to move a little way to the side again to see the things in perspective, but once he did, there was no doubt. Anchored somehow in the channel bottom—perhaps driven down into solid rock beneath a layer of sand and silt— were three metal stakes with looped tops. Certainly, an arrangement for tying down something!

He let the boat sink to the water, where it bobbed with the swell. He stared toward the island. As well as he could judge, this was at the right angle from the beach where he'd spied upon the Onsians and seen Gondal emerge.

Assume this was the spot. What had Gondal moored here? Why did it need mooring? A surface boat? No, too visible to any patrol or chance Vreddan traffic. A submersible of some kind? If so, why a tie-down? Could it not simply rest on the bottom?

He remembered the violent storms here.

So the Onsian pirate had probably moored some kind of a vehicle here, submerged. Where was it now? Vince peered down. Gradually, he made out marks in the sand. Something oblong had rested there. No drag-marks led away from the spot, so whatever it was had risen upward before moving laterally.

It seemed entirely possible that Gondal, with his connections and his daring, could smuggle a small shuttleboat onto Shann, or, possibly, by means of adequate bribes or coercion, procure one here. All right, that was as good a guess as Vince could make here and now. The Onsian wanted to be able to move about unbeknownst to the Vred. A risky thing, but, given all the electronic and other counter-measures available to Gondal, no riskier, certainly, than Vince's current sortie. He stared again toward the island. Probably some patrol or other had passed over the small beach he'd quitted, by now, and Central would be sure he'd moved. Not having any report from him, as he'd promised, nor any radar record, what would they assume? That he'd forgotten, and crossed the island low down so he didn't show? Hardly. They'd consider that possibility, but also others closer to the truth. He'd better not stay here!

Should he try to sneak back to the beach; claim, if asked, that he'd merely hopped along the surf for a few minutes, seeking a better spot? He thought he had a fair chance of getting away with that.

But he'd come out here to learn what Gondal had up his sleeve. Gondal clearly kept some sort of vehicle here. And it was gone at the moment, which meant that. . . .

He stared toward the mainland. And presently his eyes fixed on a certain spot: one of the higher, though not the highest, of the peaks along the coast. To Vince's eyes the whole peak glowed with a faint, familiar, purple-blue light!

Insides kneading, he put the boat to skimming across the channel. He didn't let himself dwell upon the foolhardiness of it except to mutter, when he was within a mile or two of the coast, "Well, the fat's in the fire now!" The English sounded odd, after talking and thinking in Lenjan for so long.

The glow from the mountain was plainer now. Could it be simply the mysterious thing Zarpi had planted? If it were extremely valuable, it had probably been transferred from the island by now.

No, even his weird eyesight couldn't perceive infinitely weak light, and this came diffusedly from the whole mountain. Whatever it was, it was vastly greater than Zarpi's device.

At least, though, there was a strong chance that it marked the Vreddan cache! Whatever the glow was (and most probably they were unaware of it) none of the other mountains showed such a thing.

He let his boat hover low while he studied the area. To the west of the mountain was a cleft, as if a river or a fjord ran down to the sea there. As well as he could make out, the mountain shoulder dropped quite steeply to that inlet. He couldn't see beyond, as the fjord, if it were one, curved; but he could see other mountains forming a background at some distance.

Meanwhile, he might as well be ashore as here! Better—he could possibly find some place to hide the shuttleboat from radar or from Vreddan eyes. It wasn't a comfortable thought, being stuck on the wild mainland, but conceivably he could find some way of sneaking back later, and cook up some story. He felt entitled to guess that Gondal would be somewhere about. Like looking for a needle in a haystack—but Vince searched with no ordinary eyes. If he found Gondal, there was the faint hope that, spying upon the pirate, he could learn some way out of this fix.

He moved on again toward the faintly glowing mountain.

Vince eased the shuttleboat in cautiously under the spreading foliage of a tree not unlike an especially leafy Terran oak. He felt like a lone soldier suddenly cut off behind enemy lines. But it was all his own doing!

There was no doubt now that he was somewhere along the way to, if not actually near, the Vreddan cache. Shuttleboats (the kind that perpetually streamed to and from the meat-processing center) came at intervals across the channel, headed up the fjord, and vanished west of the mountain. How far they went he had no way of guessing. Certainly, he wasn't going to try to follow one—he'd blaze on radar-screens like a nova. He didn't even dare fly around the mountain to a better spying-spot, since it was more than probable they'd have a thorough watch there.

He stared across the channel toward the colony. The air was hazy just now, but he could see the glow of light around the field. He daren't separate the boat from the mountain's mass by more than a few yards. He'd come up here, almost brushing the jungled slope, because he'd seen from a little way out that the jungle gave way, a mile or so up, to scattered trees and grassy patches. Now that he was here, he doubted that he could hedgehop around the mountain, or over it, without being detected. Another instance of his planning! So, unless he wanted to give up, he faced the necessity of leaving the shuttleboat and reconnoitering on foot.

He sat there a few minutes longer, watching another Vreddan boat come lining into sight (three or four thousand feet lower than he) and vanish up the fjord. So far, he hadn't seen any animal life this high on the mountain except some rabbitlike things with the saucer-eyes that seemed to be usual on Shann. Still, those small animals moved with a caution that suggested bigger ones.

And he had no weapon except a knife or whatever he could fashion from the fishing gear.

Fuming inwardly at himself for launching into a thing like this without a little preparation, he turned in the seat and fumbled among the gear; he chose a fairly bulky fishing-pole handle and hoisted it doubtfully. Not as heavy as a baseball bat, but he could jab with it, if necessary.

Just as he was about to open the hatch and climb out, a movement to one side caught his eye. A long, short-legged quadruped somewhat bigger than a dachshund scuttled across the open, crouched in the blue-black grass, and finally slunk out of sight behind a treetrunk.

He hesitated, shrugged, opened the hatch, and climbed out. For a minute he stood peering about and listening. He tried to form a picture of the surroundings so he could find his way back to the boat (though he had no idea what he'd do if he *did* get back to it), then moved quietly to the base of a tree. Another pause brought no hint of danger.

He set off around the slope, moving from one isolated treetrunk to another when he could, avoiding the patches of underbrush as much as possible, crouching at the edge of each open grassplot to listen and peer around. Once something snarled hoarsely from a tree limb just over his head. He leaped aside, inadequate club raised, but the creature looked no more dangerous than a house cat. It had ears almost the size of his palm, and big, round eyes that stared at him unblinkingly.

Before he'd gone a mile he'd flushed a dozen of the rabbity things and two of the long-bodied, short-legged creatures. He'd also seen several more of the catlike things. The fur color of everything tended to dark gray, with slight patterning of a lighter hue that, perhaps, helped as camouflage. He saw no bright colors except when a single bird went swooping across his path and down-slope.

He moved on around the mountain more confidently. Now and then there was a roar or a screech from lower down, within the jungle's fringe, but nothing came up into sight. He began to hope he'd been lucky enough to land in a safe zone.

Starlight glittered from the surface of the fjord a half-mile below him. Obviously the seawater reached several miles inland, at least (the inlet curved north of the mountain), but, judging from what he could see of it, a river-canyon must empty into it. On the other side of the fjord, peaks lower than the one above him but still high enough to thrust above the jungle, formed a serrated wall.

A shuttleboat came into sight between two of those peaks, a broad cone of light fanning out ahead of it. He watched it slant down until it was within five hundred feet or so of the water, then turn down-fjord, joining the regular flyway. A genuine hunting party, he decided, returning with its bag. He'd been sitting here, hidden in a small thicket, for half an hour, and hadn't seen a single boat fly on up the fjord or return from there. All (he tallied nine so far) turned off at one point or another, mounted the western wall of the chasm, and disappeared into the country beyond.

He was beginning to fume at himself again. Had he been wrong after all? But he'd come too far, risked too much, to give up so quickly.

And in twenty more minutes he saw what he'd been watching for.

A shuttleboat arriving from the direction of the colony paused, hovered, then moved slowly westward across the fjord, losing altitude as it went. Its light swept the water ahead of it as if it were, perhaps, following a school of fish or a single swerving sea-animal. Finally it landed and extinguished all its lights. Though the distance from him by now was considerable, he thought he could make out movement as if fishing gear were being broken out.

Minutes passed. Then he was sure that the boat had buttoned up again, with all its crew inside it. It began to move slowly, so close to the water he wouldn't have known it had taken off except that he saw no bow wave ahead of it and no wake behind.

It slanted up and across toward his side of the fjord, finally vanishing around the sheer shoulder of the mountain. It turned on no lights.

His pulse was hot and loud in his temples. This might still be, he told himself, a legitimate hunting foray, but he was going on around the mountain and see!

He started on, and met a new problem. This north side of the mountain seemed considerably moister, with correspondingly thicker vegetation. He avoided the jungle by moving a little higher; but the oak-shaped trees grew more thickly, and various kinds of brush closed the spaces between them. He'd expected the inland side of the mountain to be drier—but of course this wasn't Earth.

He gripped his makeshift weapon and moved on.

Suddenly a rope settled over his shoulders.

Vince grabbed at the rope, but it was quickly jerked tight. Someone (or something!) gave a mighty tug that pulled him off his feet. He tumbled, struggling, down the slope, brought up jarringly against a treetrunk. Then big gray-furred bipeds converged on him and pinned him down. He fought, but their weight was crushing, their big thick-fingered hands too strong.

Finally he lay gasping for breath and trembling with fury and exhaustion while they trussed him expertly. He knew by now that his captors were ipsisumoedans. What a fool! He'd been fretting over the possibility of dangerous carnivores, wishing he had a heavier club, and had completely forgotten that there were intelligent natives on Shann!

Sullenly, he got to his feet under their not-too-rough but maddeningly assured prodding and let himself be urged down-slope into the unreassuring dark fringes of the jungle.

There was a certain amount of hushed talk between his captors, in a language that sounded outlandish to him, but seemed very complex, involving long words or phrases and a staggering variety of sounds. There were also exchanges with unseen pickets. And, when they'd penetrated perhaps two hundred yards down into the jungle, he began to see a glow ahead—brighter, perhaps, than the starlight which was now almost totally cut off by the canopy overhead.

His captors pushed him indifferently into a clearing.

He stood for a minute, rooted where they let go of him, staring like a child at the fantastic scene.

The light came from four small animals, similar, he thought, to the catlike ones he'd been seeing, but obviously tame. Each seemed to have luminous skin on the fronts of its ears, chest, and forelegs. He gaped. Each of the beasts was cradled in the arms of an ipsisumoedan standing at one of the four points of the compass. The thought moved vaguely through his benumbed mind that they could hardly be aware of directions, since Shann had no sun; then he remembered that Shann *did* rotate, and that even primitives are familiar with the wheeling of the stars. The four huge bipeds stroked the animals gently, their big hands ludicrously careful, and now and then crooned to them in deep, soft voices. The beasts seemed ready to purr, though Vince heard no such sound.

Seated with their backs against treetrunks were an arc of the big furred warriors, their old ear-tentacles quirking. Vince shivered involuntarily. The ipsisumoedans stared at him, motionless except for that tentacle-quirking and an occasional slow blink of a long, narrow eye.

He noted, this time for sure, that they did have slit pupils (widened, now, into ovals). He realized from the way they peered at him that the light was none too ample for them.

One of the four animals being stroked uttered a small sound like the chittering of a sleepy squirrel. The native holding it put it down gently, gave it a pat, and let it trot away into the jungle. Vince noticed with amazement that the glow vanished abruptly from the small creature's forward-facing patches of skin.

The ipsisumoedan called gutterally, and an answering animal-like call came from somewhere nearby. Another of the small beasts bounded into sight, its foreparts already beginning to glow, and leaped into the big biped's arms. From a pouch at his belt, the native got a bit of meat and offered it to the creature, which ate daintily, then settled down to be stroked, its glow steady.

So the natives tamed animals that had something of the propensity of glowworms. A good arrangement, especially as the living lamp could prowl off and fend for itself when necessary!

One of the squatting natives, dressed only in loincloth

and belt like the others, but fondling a spear with some-what ornate shaft-carving, suddenly spoke in perfect Lenjan. "I have seen you before, I think! What is your species called?"

Vince jumped a little, then stared at the speaker for a moment before collecting his wits. "I—we are called Carcans, after our original world. I'm a guest on the island. Why have you—Why did your men seize me like this?"

The only-moderately large mouth opened briefly in a grin. Vince noted that the teeth weren't carnivorous, though they might easily be omnivorous. "A guest on the island, Carcan? An amusing statement. I apologize if my warriors were rough with you—more heartily since I am indebted to you. You saved my life not long ago."

Vince gaped. This was too much of a coincidence! Was he gripped in some vivid nightmare? "You—you're the same one?"

The ear-tentacles curled and uncurled in what might be an affirmative. "My name is Gingranibren. As second son of Chief Hakoor, I lead spying expeditions, which, in this part of the world, are mostly directed against the Vred. It was a very fortunate thing that you happened to be hovering overhead when I stupidly allowed myself to be stalked. Though not entirely coincidental, I think, as you and I were at that moment spying upon something of mutual interest! As to your finding me again here on the flank of Weeping Woman, that is no miracle either. I spend much time here." He sat eyeing Vince (as, Vince thought, a well-fed cat might eye an interesting new kind of mouse). "You seem to see quite well by this feeble light we dare here. Yet your eyes are no larger than those of the Vred. And on the other occasion you were able to see me and the kantabeleen, though both of us were partly screened from you by foliage. Do you, then, possess unheard-of dark-vision?"

Vince stiffened involuntarily. Cold insect feet walked up his spine. This primitive had a mind like a razor! He thought frantically. "I, uh, do have fair dark-vision. And there are, you know, instruments that enable one to see by . . . by light that is ordinarily invisible."

The tentacles half coiled. "So I have heard. Perhaps you are wearing one now? No matter. I am inclined to think we are not enemies, Carcan. You were furtively spying upon Gondal." The gray-furred humanoid grinned at Vince's start. "Yes, I know of him. And you have come here, in perilous evasion of the Vred, to spy upon *them*. There are things, I do not doubt, that you could tell us. Understand, we are not at war with the Vred, but neither are we allied with them. We have reason to spy also upon the pirate Gondal. *You* appear to have reason to spy upon both. Should we not consider exchanging information?"

Vince stood unhappily silent. His stomach felt as if something heavy and indigestible were balled up in it. Obviously he had to avoid angering these natives. He sighed. "My reason for spying upon Gondal is a directly personal one. As to my other activities . . ."

Gingranibren smiled. "I see no need to torture information out of you at the moment. Perhaps we can agree upon this much: Neither of us will betray the other to the Vred. As for Gondal, if *you* will not tell him that *I* have spied upon him, *I* will not tell him that *you* have done so. Do you find that reasonable?"

Vince stared at the furry being. Presently he could not help grinning. "Yes, I do." He sobered. "Not that I expect ever to see Gondal again."

Gingranibren smiled with evident deep amusement. "That is as the Die Casters arrange. Meanwhile, we cannot stay here. We will untie you, but weapons will be ready. We have an hour's travel."

Vince opened his mouth to demand where they were going, to protest that his shuttleboat was unguarded. He decided to say nothing. The boat might be a hole card later.

The way they took slanted farther around to the north and a little down the jungle slope. There were game trails, or perhaps native trails. There seemed to be no dangerous wildlife about. Perhaps the ipsisumoedans, or the Vred, kept it away from this side of the mountain.

From time to time they passed sentries.

The trail wasn't easy. They climbed across vast rock outcroppings, dipped into ravines. Once they went hand-over-hand along jungle vines that seemed to festoon themselves naturally from tree to tree. Eventually, though, they reached another cavern-like clearing where sentries passed them, and where warriors stood stroking the catlike beasts to make them glow.

Vince stopped, dumbfounded and dismayed.

There was a medium-sized shuttleboat in the clearing, one of the spaceworthy (and submersible!) models. And, sprawled casually on the leaf-littered ground, one snakehead chewing absently at a roasted leg of some small animal, while his breathing-appendage took leisurely drags from his back-cannister, was Gondal.

CHAPTER FOURTEEN

VINCE, unwilling to show the dismay he felt, stood sullenly facing the many-limbed Onsian. Finally he said, "So you've managed to corrupt the natives too. Quite a stable you keep! Thood Hivvis, some Vreddan official or other to get that shuttleboat, whatever spies you've got around the colony, me, and Shann's natives."

Gondal casually uncoupled his breathing-appendage from the cannister. "Hiss-hiss-hiss. You forget to mention spies among the Nesse, though I have not been too successful there. I am a comparatively small entrepreneur, really. And there is some element on Shann just now, which I've been totally unable to crack, that worries me. To translate a saying of my own race, there is a strange taste in the currents."

Vince glanced at Gingranibren. The big demi-humanoid was watching him intently, hearing-tentacles rigid and slightly inclined toward him, an expression of wary amusement on his furry face. Vince thought bitterly of the promise they'd exchanged: not to betray one another to Gondal—No! That hadn't been it, precisely. The pact, as it related to the Onsian, mentioned only one specific point. Vince found himself grinning with admiration. The native was sharp! And, as Gingranibren had obviously foreseen, the pact was still mutually necessary. He faced Gondal again. "You mean there's a base you haven't covered? Surely, with your talents—"

Gondal waved a tentacle. "It is no fit subject for jokes. Had you ever been caught aground and unarmored during a raid upon a planet, you would. . . . But let us not borrow trouble. Since we are here, shall we finally place trust in one another? How did you find this mountain? And how did you evade the proprietors and get here?"

Vince allowed himself a grin. "I waited until they were looking the other way, then I swam. How did *you* get here?"

Gondal gestured impatiently. "Don't be a clown. It is your time you are wasting, as well as mine. I suppose you rented a shuttleboat, flew up-island, then came across low on the water. How did you locate the mountain?"

Vince thought hard. The only information he must withhold was the very faint glow of the mountain. "Locating the place isn't hard. It's the only direction where there's a consistent flow of traffic. The Vred pretend it's just a stream of hunters moving to and from the mainland to keep the meat-butchers supplied. But if you watch closely, there's too much."

Gondal sighed. "It took me hundreds of hours analyzing radar-tapes to learn that. You see how useful those eyes of yours are?"

There was a chuckle from Gingranibren. Gondal glanced at the native and shrugged. "It may as well be revealed. This being—Vinz Kul Lo, if you haven't already exchanged names—has a pair of very specially modified eyes. I procured that modification for him, though without his consent, and now I control his continued eyesight. Let us state our community of interests. Geegee and his people would like to see the Vred leave Shann. Vinz Kul Lo wants to continue seeing, and may, though he declines to admit it so far, also share the greed that is *my* motivation. If we are able to penetrate and burglarize the Vreddan treasury, all of us will have advanced toward our goals. Can we not agree to pool our resources and efforts?"

Geegee, still looking amused, said, "Onsian, you and my father have already reached agreement. We will not, except in self-defense, fight hopelessly against Vreddan weapons. We *will* spy for you, and give you such help as we prudently can."

Gondal waved a tentacle. "A sound agreement, and there

is yet no reason to alter it. Vinz, *you* are the surly one."

Vince sighed. "*You* arranged both sides of my relationship with you."

Gondal heaved his bulk impatiently. "So you still refuse to confide in me further about the Nesse, including Zarpi. Very well—that may endanger all of us, but we'll be neglectful if you insist. You did not come to this mountain, and begin to explore around it, without theories. How do you think we might go about locating the actual cache?"

"My theories," Vince told him, "don't amount to much so far. All I know is, a certain number of shuttleboats darken completely, rest on the water for a few minutes, then move on, very low, up the inlet. I suppose you've already gone farther than that."

Gondal tensed a little and hissed something in his own language. "I had not. It is impossible, you understand, to bring equipment in here for a radar-scan, without being caught. They move on around the mountain?"

"So far as I was able to see before our furry partners here caught me."

Gondal got to his four leg-tentacles and moved about impatiently. "Then the search has only begun. I came here, a few hours ago, merely to meet Geegee and hear his reports. When you appeared, I had hopes you had learned something. And we may not have much time—surely they have discovered your absence by now. I wish you had confided in me! I could have arranged some way. . . . But that is empty seashells now. I suppose we must move on foot around the mountain. Geegee? You will have to guide."

The trail they took this time was less strenuous, but even more indirect. They veered up out of the jungle to avoid an impenetrable stretch, then down into it again, crossed ravines and detoured around spots that Geegee said held Vreddan watch-posts. Now and then Vince had glimpses of the fjord far below them. Once he saw a shuttleboat moving steadily up it, very near this side. He alerted his companion and watched it as long as it was in sight.

It was only minutes later that movement in the sky brought him to a sudden halt. Geegee, watching him closely, muttered something to Gondal.

Vince crouched against a treetrunk, staring up through the foliage. Then, slowly, he straightened.

"What was it?" Gondal demanded quietly.

"A shuttleboat. One of the model you, ah, acquired. It was slanting down from the top of the mountain. Maybe it was a genuine hunting party."

Geegee said in a very low voice, "By treaty, they do not hunt on this side of the inlet. We must try not to be noisy. They have listening devices when they fly over like that. They are surely seeking intruders." In what to him was near-darkness, his eyes turned to Vince. "Are you sure you were not followed?"

Vince shrugged. "All I can guarantee is that I can see as well by starlight as—well, as you see by a torch, if you ever use them. Nothing visible followed me. Radar passed over me, but I doubt that it registered me against the backgrounds."

Gondal crouched, snakeheads arrested as he thought. "Geegee, how close are we to those cliffs you described?"

"A half-hour's travel. We had better not go to the edge, I think. Slight noises, or the presence of body heat, they will not find unusual. We hunt near there regularly, and there are animals. But if a party appeared on the brink of the cliffs . . ."

Gondal cursed in Onsian. "Well, can you find us a spot where we can watch the inlet?"

"That I can do, though it will mean an hour's extra travel. Perhaps it is worthwhile, if Vinz Kul Lo's eyes are sensitive enough to see everything upon the water. We have often seen Vreddan flying-boxes fishing along the fjord, and sometimes they darken their lights. But we have never seen any large amount of traffic."

Gondal said, "They could come in to this part of the inlet submerged, except for a few that show themselves to ward off suspicion. Well . . ."

They moved on along the fringe of the jungle. Twenty minutes or so passed.

Then, suddenly, the universe seemed to drown in blinding light.

Vince clutched at the treetrunk beside which he'd been standing. For a moment he wondered if he were blind, then his eyes began to adjust again to the dark. He realized that the sudden burst of light hadn't really been all that intense—it was just the sensation; and his marvelous artificial lens—wafers had cut it down, in any case, to bearable proportions.

And then he realized that the others around him were not even temporarily dazzled, though they crouched in arrested positions, staring upward. To them, the flash must have been mild!

Geegee regained composure quickly. "A meteor, heading straight down? I saw no streak—"

Gondal was gliding fluidly into deeper cover. "No meteor —that was a ship being blasted into particles, far above atmosphere!" His heads swiveled toward Vince. "Now is no time for coyness, tyro! Speak! Have you any hint of a Nessen plan to invade here? That was no Vreddan weapon! They would not use a type that would set off a ship's fissionables—the flash would be visible too far. We are caught in the open. Speak!"

Vince stood scowling at the Onsian. "There was no such hint. I—damn it—I was supposed just to inform them when Zarpi and Akorra were here, and try to infiltrate Zarpi's crew if I could. There was an artifact involved that the Nesse wanted back very badly. I'm *sure* they wouldn't risk destroying it, along with Akorra!"

Gondal's four small eyes peered toward him beadily. "Ah! An artifact! Lenjan, no doubt. Things become slightly less murky. . . . The Nesse wanted to recover both the artifact and the female scientist. Tell me this, Vinz Kul Lo, have you already alerted the Nesse that Zarpi is here? Did they, after all, provide you with some way of reporting, even without a message-drone?"

Vince hesitated unwillingly. In that moment there was another flash in the sky, a faint one this time, as if some terrific detonation had occurred far around the planet, with only the ghost of it reflected here by the atmosphere. There *must* be an invasion under way! "I—yes, I've already reported Zarpi's presence, and when I saw Akorra I reported that too. But the—the technique doesn't allow complex messages. That was why—" He went silent abruptly, staring up through the foliage.

"What is it?" Gondal hissed.

"I'm not sure. A silhouette against the stars, very low. It must have hedgehopped the peak of this mountain. One of Zarpi's ships, I think!"

Gondal hissed angrily. "Then he too has pinpointed this place—and he's suddenly desperate, as we are." The Onsian's heads darted toward Geegee. "Quickly! To where we can see the inlet!"

But Vince was seeing more movement through the foliage. "I doubt that it's much use now! Shuttleboats are going over—dozens of them! I'd guess, wouldn't you, that the Vred are preparing to load what they can and evacuate? This invasion—whoever it is—how soon will it land? How much time do we have? Maybe we can get back to the island and—"

Gondal's breathing-appendage shot toward him. "Fool! Do you think I'm going to abandon the greatest treasure ever assembled—not to mention a Lenjan artifact of inestimable value, if you're finally telling the truth—when I'm standing right on top of it? The invasion will have this world cordoned in; but with any luck at all, my ship and crew will have broken orbit and escaped. The Vred, except for a diversionary flight or two, will not yet try to escape. They will load the best of the treasury and wait for the right moment—I have assurance of this. Possibly they already have ships loaded somewhere, hidden, ready to take off later. They may have other tricks up their sleeves too. do not doubt—"

There was a heavy explosion that made the mountain

tremble. Gondal hissed in rage. "A ship's rupter! Zarpi, the fool! He'll bring the invasion right down to this spot! Damnation! To be caught here, without resources!" He darted furious looks at Geegee. *"Will* you get us to that spot?"

The ipsisumoedan stood, arms folded across his chest, massively calm, his quick mind no doubt running through the dangers and possible consequences. He paid Gondal no attention except a flick or two of a hearing-organ.

The Onsian moved his bulk ominously toward the native, producing from somewhere a handgun of some kind. There might have been a senseless clash, but Vince, standing beneath a break in the foliage and peering upward, stopped it. "Hold on. Ships are already coming down!"

Gondal spun toward him. "What kind are they? Do you recognize them?"

"Yes, I recognize them." Vince felt a dull sickness in his middle. "Dumbbell-shaped vessels. Chullwei."

And now Geegee suddenly spoke. "They'll have zeroed in on this mountain, if they are already in atmosphere— that local detonation was enough, was it not? Partners in peril, there are things I have not told you. I reveal them now, not because of logic, but because my hunch-cog grinds at me. This mountain is indeed hollow, or partly so! There are ancient entrances, well hidden, that my people have known of for generations. And others, I do not doubt, that have never been found. We have never explored them, because of the Vred occupation and the certainty that Vred have another entrance and often use it. They do not know of these upper entrances, we think, and only use passage-ways deep in the mountain. Think, partners: here we are, seized up in a great drama. Should we not play out our parts? And do not those parts call for us to explore one of these ancient entrances? Or should we wait here like insects for the weapons of the invaders or of the Vred to incinerate us?"

Gondal was hissing frantically. "Of *course* we shall play out our parts! Lead! Lead!"

Fifteen minutes later, after a breathless climb, Geegee pushed into a thicket, led the way to an overgrown pile of rocks, and began hastily tossing those aside. "There is a metal grill here, through which air of perceptible warmth has been felt to rise. The grill, though corroded, is still very strong. Gondal, that hand weapon of yours—"

The Onsian had already joined Geegee and several of his warriors at the task. Vince, moving a rock or two, saw the pattern of the grill begin to emerge. "Why, it's vertical, set in a pit! It'll be flooded!"

Geegee paused to reply. "Not so, outworlder. There is a cunning drainage system that empties this pit. . . . There, see the top hinge of the grill?"

Vince pushed close. "Space, it's old! We'll have to cut around it." Vince grabbed more rocks and tossed them out. "The latch. . . . No, I don't think there ever was a latch— it was simply welded shut!"

Presently the pit was empty enough. Gondal squeezed himself impatiently forward. "Kul Lo, show me the weakest places to cut! We don't want to leave obvious signs."

Vince, shielding his eyes from the bright sparks, stood aside with Geegee. "We're going to leave an obvious trail here!"

Geegee chuckled. "Some of my warriors will pile the rocks back once we're inside, and straighten up the surroundings. Are you frightened, Vinz Kul Lo, at entering a dark hole that leads to something unpredictable?"

Vince grinned. "Frightened? I'm scared weak! But with those Chullwei coming down, a dark hole sounds pretty good by comparison!"

The hinges and sealing-weld were cut around now. Gondal wrapped tentacles around bars of the grill, heaved, and grunted. "It is stuck tight, of course! After all these centuries—"

Geegee suggested softly, "Warm the crack all around, then let it cool."

Gondal darted a snakehead toward the native, hissed something, and followed the suggestion.

The grill, under combined efforts, finally tore loose

with a sound as if the roots of the mountain were coming up.

Vince stood staring into the dark hole. "I have something to contribute. This mountain glows all over—faintly, but enough for me to see. The same glow seems to exist in this tunnel; it's a spill from energy of some kind stored in the mountain. Better let me lead!"

The bore was about eight feet high and half as wide, flat-floored, rounded at the top. There was a certain amount of distortion around the mouth, where stalactites and stalagmites had formed from water seeping in, but beyond that, the walls were completely smooth and without aggregation of any kind. There must be a lining completely impervious to water.

Twenty-five yards into the mountain the tunnel turned sharply. A routine arrangement, of course, to guard against blast-penetraton. Presently there was another turn, then the faintly glowing bore stretched straight on into the mountain. Now it slanted downward.

He could hear the others groping their way behind him. As his eyes made final adjustment, he could see quite well. He paused. "Why doesn't one of you put a hand on my shoulder, and follow close behind?"

There were murmurs of agreement—the blackness must be very uncomfortable for the others. But it was one of Gondal's tentacles that draped itself lightly over Vince's shoulder. He suppressed a shudder and led on.

It was shortly after that when the mountain shook with a series of detonations. The quivering, and subsequent rumbling, seemed to come from below. Vince cringed, half expecting the tunnel to collapse on them. But Gondal, whose faintly ammoniacal breath was about Vince now, hissed angrily, "That Zarpi! Unless I am wrong, he has located the Vreddan entrance and is fighting his way in. Well, the drama sharpens, eh? Here we are, headed downward—almost unarmed, but with surprise on our side—and Zarpi enters from below. Between, the Vred must wait, with or without ample resources of their own. And meanwhile, the Chullwei, unquestionably in overwhelming force, are about to land!"

Vince looked back at the party. Besides him and Gondal there were Geegee and six ipsisumoedan warriors, armed with spears and knives. A brief nervous laugh escaped him, then he led on down the tunnel.

The ever descending bore was joined by others, including some that must be no more than ventilation shafts. There were occasional cracks in the lining, but only one place where an earthquake had significantly broken the tunnel, so that the party had to squeeze through. For a ways below that, of course, the debris covered the floor; but the air was not damp. There must be ancient machinery still at work, removing moisture.

There were faint but steady sounds of combat from below, but no more blasting for a while. There were remoter detonations which Gondal judged to be the Chullwei overcoming token resistance in the air. The Vred must feel brutally beleaguered: their secret cache ferreted out and invaded, the colony overwhelmed by another enemy.

Vince worried about what might be happening on the island. Was the field being blasted to rubble? Was his own ship, along with the hundreds of others, destroyed? What about the supply of medicine for his eyes? Where had Gondal hidden that, and what had happened to it now?

Of course, he thought wryly, he might not have to worry that far ahead.

His thoughts moved to other things, and finally he decided to confide a little more in Gondal. "There's one thing that puzzles me. Zarpi was supposed to be dickering, somehow, with the Chullwei. How does that fit events here?"

"Hiss-hiss-hiss! No great surprise to me. He has been double-crossed, perhaps, and outwitted. I have little concern for his pale-furred hide—I am more worried about my own! I, Vinz Kul Lo, am as badly marooned now as you—except for a few insignificant gadgets I have hidden out on Shann, and those are unreachable at the moment.

Have you been comprehending the sounds from below in the last few minutes?"

"No, except that it sounds as if either Zarpi or the Vred are mopping up."

"The mopping up, I judge, is already completed, except possibly for lurking bands of defenders. For the last ten minutes there has been a skirling sound, punctuated by tremors and rattles and booms. If I interpret it right, a heavy beamer and some rupter-rifles are at work, boring through rock. Zarpi, then, is trying to reach something that stirs his greed as much or more than the Vreddan treasury, which he must have taken by now. He cannot, of course, merely fight his way back out of whatever chambers lie below; he knows by now that the Chullwei have landed. What has he in mind? Remember, Akorra has been in his hands for some time. Has he extracted from her knowledge of some vital Lenjan installation—here, in this mountain?" The Onsian was silent for a while except for the intermittent hiss of his breathing. "What of the tunnel, Vinz Kul Lo? It feels unchanged. Are there any signs of artifacts?"

"No. Why don't you make a light? That hand-beamer of yours will do it."

"Of course. But an energy-discharge here might be detectable, and there's no need to risk it while you lead."

"Oh. Well, there's no change. No openings but ventilation holes. What would you expect?"

Gondal said, "This is Lenjan work, of course; no known technology bored this tunnel, and lined it so lastingly. I have been vaguely hoping we might find Lenjan weapons, left behind in the evacuation. Even a ship or some other sort of conveyance. Hiss-hiss-hiss! I am like a child in trouble, hoping for miraculous rescue. Geegee, perhaps you have more knowledge of which you can unburden yourself. Do your people have legends of ancient occupation of this planet?"

"We do not, Onsian. There are ruins of great antiquity in various parts of the planet. There is one almost-vanished installation near a string of old volcanoes in the northern part of this continent, the purpose of which we speculate to have been the extraction of what you call "fissionables" from the magma that welled up. Those are many, many thousands of cycles old. It is only since the coming of the Vred that we have learned Lenjan speech, and something of sciences such as archeology. Before that, we were primitive and ignorant." Geegee chuckled in the darkness. "Even more so than now."

Gondal said, "A pity. Well, the Lenj were obviously here, but I begin to despair that these tunnels hold anything for us! We have been spiraling down for thousands of feet with no encouragement—except that we approach nearer to Zarpi, who must be counted a deadly enemy. If there were anythng useful inside the mountain, by now we should—"

Vince interrupted with a low exclamation. "Maybe you're speaking too soon! The tunnel continues on straight for about a hundred yards, and I can see others branching off it. Dead ahead is a chamber of some kind, with—with objects in it. The glow is stronger from there. *Can't you see it?*"

For a moment there was silence except for the breathing of various members of the party. Then Geegee said very softly, "Now that I know where to look, I can see, or imagine, a very faint outline!"

There were hissing sounds and a thump as if Gondal were getting himself a hasty lungful of air. "Silently, then, from here! Kul Lo, pause just outside the chamber and peer before you enter. We are very vulnerable!"

CHAPTER FIFTEEN

THE GROUP, convinced there was no immediate threat, stood silently staring, just inside the chamber. Vince wondered if the others, waiting there blindly for him to describe things, felt the same prickling awe he did.

Not that there was anything understandably frightening about the array of machinery that lined one wall, rather, Vince realized, the awe arose in his own mind from the sense of the time-lapse since this place was abandoned by its builders. Then, too, there was the fear-reaction to the strange, for he had not the slightest notion what he was looking at.

What, for instance, was the function of a cluster of translucent hexahedrons—a hundred or more of them, all volleyball-sized, forming together an elongated irregular figure that stood erect like some gigantic granular worm, inside a cage of loosely meshed crisscross wires? Or of a horizontal disc near the ceiling, six feet across, perforated irregularly by small holes, encircled about its periphery by what seemed to be a complex toroidal coil of heavy wire or tubing? Or of a ten-foot gray sphere with irregular etching upon it, balanced upon three ball-rollers atop a boxlike structure—and with twenty or more electrodes, on the ends of curling pipes, pointing at it?

Vince realized suddenly that the sphere might represent a world—Shann, for instance—and that the electrodes might illuminate various points of it as it was turned about, or beam strange energies upon it, or take readings from it. The etching could represent seas and continents. . . .

Even less comprehensible was the bank of slots, each

with toggle-switches above and below them. Or—could those slots accept Lenj coins? They could, he decided. From here he couldn't read the Lenjan script below each slot.

But the double row of dial gauges above the bank of slots and toggles looked as familiar as the rest of the things were strange. Dials to register what?

Gondal hissed agitatedly, "Space, Kul Lo! Describe what you see!"

Vince took a deep breath, and realized he'd been needing it. "Well—"

But at that moment Geegee chuckled, reached into his belt-pouch, and drew out something like a very large kitchen-match. He turned and scratched it against the wall, then had to scratch again on the smooth surface before it burst into flame. "I do not think, Gondal, that lucifer-torches will register on the electronic instruments you fear."

"Hiss! Good! Have you more of those?"

Two warriors produced the things and lighted them. The party moved across the chamber, taking the island of illumination with them.

Gondal crouched, breathing noisily. "The gods! There must have been a fantastic amount of machinery controlled from here—Look at those switches and dials!" The Onsian accepted a lucifer-torch from Geegee and glided hastily toward the gray sphere. "See, a globe-map! Who knows what might be projected upon it, to be observed from here?"

Vince led them down to the cluster of hexagons. "What do you make of this?"

Gondal hissed uncertainly for a minute, then let out his breath in a long sigh. "Space! Can it be. . . . Yes, I swear—I'll bet my holdings on it—that is a mockup of the Lenjan empire! Not only in this cell, but in all of the galaxy! Each of those hexahedrons—have we gone astray in thinking of cells as spheres?—must represent a cell! Each could be lighted, perhaps—or many of them—to show location, while a voice message was heard—"

"Why," Vince asked him, "is it in a frail-looking cage like that? An energy-field of some sort around it?"

"Eh? Oh, those are essentially three sets of coils, with their axes at right angles. By a combination of currents in the three, nodes could be set up in any chosen hexahedron, to make it glow or, conversely, to read something from it. Nothing incomprehensible there. . . . Look about. Do you see anything that looks like a weapon, or a weapon-locker?"

"No. But there's another tunnel leading out of this place. To your left, there."

Gondal peered into the dimness. "Best we follow it! But extinguish the torches—and you lead again, Vinz!"

Vince trotted to get ahead. After a few seconds in the new tunnel his eyes adjusted, and he could see by the familiar glow. The tunnel had a double turn in it, for blast protection no doubt, then there was another chamber ahead. "Wait here—I'll scout!"

A minute later he was standing in another chamber, one that dwarfed the first, and felt himself atremble with excitement. For, if the first chamber was a sort of communicatons center, this one was an unmistakable travel depot! And among other things, including another of the empire-map mockups, there was a ship.

The lucifer-torches made an oasis of light in which Gondal and Geegee stood staring at a huge cage-like structure, from various points of which giant electrodes aimed inward at the ship. The ship, dimly lit by the torches, nestled in a shallow cradle at the focus of the electrodes (or whatever they were). Vince, having moved a little way from the light because he felt nervous with his dark-vision drowned out, stood in the niche between the wall and a thick column that rose clear to the ceiling. There were doors in the base of the column, all closed. He wondered if this might be an elevator shaft. The thought was disturbing, especially in conjunction with the sounds from below. There'd been one considerable jar, followed by a loud rumble, just after he'd entered this vast chamber.

Five of Geegee's warriors moved silently to take up places near the tunnel mouth, extinguishing their torches. It gave Vince a sense of security to see them peering about, their eyes passing over him unseeingly.

Another jar came from below; and this time he felt the definite trembling of the column against which he leaned. He jerked away instinctively, then, more sensibly, leaned back to put his ear against it.

Definitely, there were grinding sounds and a faint clatter as of falling rock. Suppose, he thought, this *were* an elevator shaft and Zarpi's crews were boring up through it, clearing away rubble or deliberately poured masses of concrete. In that case they'd emerge *here!*

He looked at Gondal, saw him scuttling around the vast cagework of cables, peering at the enclosed ship. The ship seemed to be made up of four—no, five—segments, each a compact cylinder, ten feet long and thirty feet in diameter. They were close-coupled, end to end, and the whole ship lay on its side on a hollow cradle.

In the visible end was a sliding door or hatch, about the size and shape of the tunnel cross section. From here he could just see a horizontal slot in that door, at about face-height. But he saw no knobs or handholds.

He could hear Gondal's excited hissing as the Onsian rubber-legged around the huge cage, holding aloft his torch. The cage would have let Gondal squeeze in anywhere, but, Vince realized, prudence forbade that. Anyway, there was a sort of entrance with an obvious control-station beside it, including a bank of instrument dials.

What Gondal hadn't seen yet, in the gloom, were five more identical cages in a row. All of them were empty.

Vince, ashamed of his urge to cower here in this nook, and seeing Gondal move toward the entrance to the occupied cage, went to join him.

Vince peered in at the ship. "All right, you say it's the tail end of the ancient evacuation, and for some reason never left. And maybe this cage, and those electrodes, could still translocate it somewhere. And suppose we were desperate enough to want to climb into it and go. To where? How would you pilot it?"

Gondal crouched for a moment as if listening to the sounds from below. "I believe I've made some headway guessing at things. Come, observe this panel here. Consider this tiny window-slot in which names appear as you turn this knob. Are they not names of places—destinations?"

Vince shrugged nervously. "Sure, it looks that way. I've been up and down the row of cages, and in each of the slots like this the same name appeared. But I don't think it's a place-name. Even if it were, what kind of a place would it be? Another city on Shann, long vanished? A planet somewhere here in the cell? Or—or some other cell of space? Maybe they had a separate name for each cell. Anyway, do you really think setting this one knob to a place-name would determine where the ship would go?"

"Hiss. Why not? There is a certain resistance of the knob to being turned, and faint thuds behind the panel as if relays were opening or closing." Gondal's two heads poked more directly at Vince. "Why do you doubt that the name you saw in all the slots is a place-name? I cannot understand that doubt."

Vince frowned at the Onsian. "Well, haven't you heard the quotation? 'Wolami lazes beneath his lamp. When the lamp is extinguished, then will Wolami gird for battle'. Does that sound like the name of a place?"

Gondal's heads weaved uncertainly. "I do not think we are justified in drawing the assumption from that. Are there not, on your own world, words which are the names of places as well as the names of individuals—or even of mythical heros? I believe that on my home world there is even an island named 'Gondal'—a small place, but on the map."

"Well, maybe so. But . . . the matter of power. How

long has this equipment been sitting here unused and untended? Can you really hope that—"

Gondal interrupted impatiently, "The gods! Many Lenjan artifacts have been dug up with their power diminished only a trifle, if at all! That means of storing power is one that scientists find most challenging—and baffling. Does not this mountain, by your own testimony, glow with some latent energy? The situation is clear enough for me: when the Lenj evacuated Shann, they left one ship behind for stragglers, fully equipped and powered and with its destination set. Those stragglers never got here. Think, Kul Lo—did Zarpi not have a specific goal in mind when he kidnapped Akorra and brought her here? And by the sounds from below that frighten us every few seconds, it appears that he is now gambling even more desperately. He made no attempt to seize Vreddan loot and escape. Does he not *know* what waits here to be found?"

Vince sighed disgustedly. "All right, I'll concede the possibility. So we're here ahead of him, and here's the ship, for the taking. *You're* the pirate, not I. *You* take the ship—I'll come along without protest. Start by opening that hatch there!"

Gondal dipped his heads sulkily. "That, I admit, is a problem. But if we are allowed time to investigate things a little . . ."

"Sure, sure! Let's investigate! I've got the eyes for the dark, I'll roam around the chamber and see what I can find, such as weapons. Meanwhile you puzzle things out here. All right?"

"Logical enough, though I am disappointed at your pessimism, Vinz Kul Lo!"

Vince wandered off. In the next half hour he found many interesting things, but few he understood, and none he felt were useful. Then there was an especially loud sound from below, and the floor shuddered. Gondal hissed, "They are getting very close! Better—there! That rapping! The elevator shaft must be cleared already!" He sent a tentacle toward Vince. "You have no weapon, Kul Lo— best stay behind me!"

Vince pulled away. "I have my eyes! Hide yourself somewhere. They'll probably have only a light or two, at first, and I'll try—"

From below, not far below, there was a sound as of ancient hinges, then a slam; then a faint scraping and humming as if—

Yes, as if an elevator were coming up the shaft!

Vince ran to the nearest bulky piece of machinery, which was the massive box atop which the gray sphere was mounted. He found space behind it and crouched to wait.

The place was dark, but Vince suddenly realized that the tarry smell of the lucifer-torches still lingered. Damn! Too late to worry about that now. With luck, it might be ignored; Zarpi might think it was ancient lubrication overheating.

He peered around. The ipsisumoedans were completely out of sight, but he could see one of Gondal's snakeheads poked blindly from cover. Vince felt a rush of anger at the Onsian. To lead them into a trap like this . . .

The scraping inside the shaft went silent. There were vague sounds and a whisper of humanoid speech, then two doors on opposite sides inched slowly open. Hinges complained. A Nessen voice cursed softly, and a second— Zarpi's—spat out a syllable to quiet the first.

The door scraped open and a Nessen stepped out, carrying a thick, stubby rupter-rifle. He placed himself with his back against the column. Another man came out the opposite door. They waited motionless for a moment, their eyes roving blindly.

From inside the column came Zarpi's muffled voice, speaking, Vince realized, from his throat mike. "We're at the next level, in a space of some kind. There's a smoky odor here, maybe from the machinery. Or maybe it's come down already from open air—the damned Chullwei may have dropped incendiaries. Look around down there for other ways up, but most of you stay near the elevator!"

118

Vince twitched. A point—the elevator could only bring up a few of the pirates at a time! But there were already two rupter-rifles in sight; and those ugly weapons could turn a man half inside out! In a closed place like this—

One door opened farther, and Akorra stumbled dazedly into sight. Behind her came Zarpi, one hand grasping her shoulder, the other holding a handgun. "Stand still," he ordered her sharply. She halted and stared about dully into the darkness, swaying a little.

Zarpi eased the weapon into a holster and took from his pocket a flashlight. "Alert!" he snapped to his men. The shaft doors were all closed now, which might or might not mean there were no more pirates inside. If not, the four Nesse were cut off alone here for the moment! But they could jerk the doors open and get back inside, and start down again.

The flashlight beam lashed out blindingly. Vince half-averted his eyes and saw the beam move slowly along the far end of the chamber; it rose to locate the ceiling, loftier than he'd realized, then moved on.

All three male Nessens gasped when the light caught the first huge installation, one of the cages. Akorra stiffened and uttered a half-incoherent cry. Something—a six-inch disc—fell from her hand and thudded on the floor.

In the frozen moment that followed there were faint sounds in the chamber, and ipsisumoedan spears flashed in the light.

Then everything seemed to burst into motion. The spears rang harshly on the elevator column. There were sudden shouts from the Nessen pirates. Rupter-rifles whipped around toward the source of the spears. Zarpi, cursing, hurled the flashlight as far from him as he could and leaped in the direction of the disc Akorra had dropped. The light struck the floor and rolled, its beam wobbling askew across a bank of machinery. Both rifle-wielders went down, one impaled through the chest by a thrown spear—but the other, grunting with pain and fury, twisted onto his side and swept his rupter in an arc, raking it across one of the huge cages. Metal shrieked and glowed. The beam evidently found the Lenjan three-dimensional map of cells, for a part of it contorted violently and Vince saw things fall. A pencil-thin beam of energy from Gondal's handgun lanced into the wounded pirate. He screamed and lay still.

Vince was already leaping toward Zarpi, who was fumbling around on the floor for the disc, but making no noise. He must have heard Vince coming, for he twisted about, grabbing for his holstered gun. Vince realized there was enough reflected light to betray him. He saw the weapon come out and swing toward him. He leaped aside desperately. Needle-bullets slammed into something and exploded. Momentarily deafened and half-blind, Vince launched himself for the disc. He fell across it as if he were recovering a football, twisted and rolled to his feet, clutching the thing. He saw ipsisumoedans converging silently, ear-organs twitching.

Zarpi was on his feet now, darting toward the elevator column, hands outstretched before him. Vince lunged to get in his way, but the Nessen fumbled for the door handle, jerked the door open, and squirmed inside. Gondal's thin beam sliced across the closing door, leaving a glowing line, but too late. Vince heard the elevator start down. Someone—Geegee, Vince thought—picked up the flashlight and aimed it this way. Vince grabbed the door handle and tugged, but the elevator had already started down and the door wouldn't open. He heard Zarpi shouting into his throat mike.

Lucifer-torches scratched and sputtered to life.

Vince turned. The ipsisumoedans were recovering their spears. Gondal, snakeheads weaving alertly, was standing beside Akorra, who rested dazedly on hands and knees.

Vince went to her. "Let me help you up!"

She submitted listlessly. Touching furred skin, Vince felt a strange half-revulsion, half-thrill. She stood unsteadily, looking about. Her eyes fixed on the map mockup and went wide. "Cells . . . a map of the cells!"

Vince felt Gondal plucking at him. "Was he wounded?" the Onsian asked excitedly.

Vince shrugged. "He may have been nicked by a spear —I wasn't sure—but no more than that." He turned back to Akorra.

She looked at him puzzledly. "Who . . . what . . ."

He showed her the disc she'd dropped. "Try to concentrate, Akorra! This thing—is it a key to the ship?"

"Ship?" She blinked at him uncomprehendingly. He turned her toward the occupied cage.

She stared, her eyes widening again. "So—so it was true! There *was* one left behind when. . . ." She took a tottering step, and Vince put an arm around her to steady her. Again, he nearly shuddered at her alien feel.

Presently the whole party was gathered around the closed hatch of the ship, watching tensely. Vince lifted the disc and held it near the slot. He'd already made sure there was a Lenj coin—no doubt one of the three he'd sold Zarpi—in the disc's own small slot. "It fits in here, doesn't it? Will it open the hatch?"

She sighed wearily. "I think . . . yes."

"And it's some kind of a program—for a certain destination, maybe?"

"I . . . it's not certain. . . ."

Gondal jabbed at him impatiently. "Time is racing!"

Vince wordlessly fitted the edge of the disc into the slot and pushed. It went in with moderate resistance about halfway, then was suddenly seized by some force, turned twenty degrees or so, and pulled home. The flat edge, still with the Lenj coin in it, filled most of the slot flush.

A second, perhaps two, passed. Then there was a whir and groan of ancient machinery and the hatch began to slide open. Lights, too bright for Vince at first, flashed on inside.

Gondal was dancing with delight. "Hiss! In with you, in with you!"

Geegee, not fitting the hatch with much to spare, picked up Akorra and hoisted her through ahead of him. Then Vince went in. Gondal grunted and hissed his way through, and finally Geegee's warriors, one by one.

There was an inner hatch, open now, forming an obvious airlock, then a space which was somewhat less than the diameter of the ship-segment, measured outside. The far bulkhead had a hatch in it identical with the one Vince had opened and that, too, was sliding open now. Vince looked along the length of the ship, seeing identical segments and hatches. He stepped into the second one. Like the first, it had wide benches, or couches; the surfaces looked soft along each side.

A voice, rather deep, a trifle halting and subtly different from any he'd ever heard, projected itself from the ceiling, though he saw no sign of a speaker-opening. "Attention. Lock will close and seal automatically in two minutes if not interrupted. Translocation begins one minute after lock seals."

Gondal jerked up both snakeheads to peer at the ceiling. "That seems to come from more than one point!"

Vince, in the second segment, said, "It's in here too!" He turned, and with midriff kneading, watched the outer door, then the inner one, slide shut. The hatches between segments remained open.

Gondal let out a nervous hiss. "I hope the seal is not defective, after so many eons! I can think of more romantic ways to die than by being exposed to space!"

CHAPTER SIXTEEN

THE LENJ had built and planned well.

That was very fortunate for Vince and his companions! For example, shortly after they were sealed in, and various dials and a recorded message told them they were under way to somewhere, Vince had the appalling realization that they'd come aboard without even thinking about food. The gods! If Vince *had* thought, he'd have assumed, naturally, that any stored food would be long since unrecognizable, let alone inedible. But there *was* food, perfectly preserved in a series of deep-freeze compartments in each segment of the ship, with machinery for getting it out and thawing it. And there was everything else an expedition might need, including garments and whole cloth, tools, hand weapons, chemicals, instruments, and various raw materials, as if the destination were unpredictable.

He discussed that with Gondal while Akorra was still asleep. He glared from one to the other of the restlessly moving snakeheads. "You must have hynotized me to get me aboard this—this elaborate coffin. From what we've found aboard so far, it looks more like a colony ship headed for some unexplored planet than like an interstellar express!"

One of Gondal's heads came to rest, its eyes regarding Vince speculatively. "I will not dispute that. Consider, though, that there were a number of destinations to choose from. We chose the one we felt the departing Lenj had chosen." The Onsian paused thoughtfully. "I am puzzled about that. One wonders whether, after all, the mere turning of a knob, as on a radio receiver, could activate computers to preset the ships' destinations."

Vince accused angrily, "You were pretty sure it could before we came aboard!"

Gondal coiled his breathing-appendage, coupled it to his back-cannister, and drew a lungful of his air-mixture before responding. "True. But I had little time to ponder. Also, there is the matter of that disc Akorra brought with her. You spoke of it as a key to open the ship, also containing a program for the ship's computers. Akorra confirmed it, more or less. You have not yet told me all you learned about it from the Nesse."

Vince stood up from the softly padded bench, or couch (which was apparently completely unaffected by its age), and paced nervously, a little awkward in the less-than-one-gee artificial gravity. "There's nothing more. They let me handle a replica of it, which is why I recognized it. Maybe both the programmed disc and the outside selector-setting were necessary."

"Possibly," Gondal said. "But maybe the knob and selector-slot had a different function. On various worlds I know, arrangements not too dissimilar dispatch message-drones, alerting far depots that ships are coming."

"Oh," said Vince bitterly, "then, if we ever reach Wolami—whatever that is—we can expect an ambush."

"Hiss-hiss-hiss. In so many thousands of years, Wolami may have moved quite a ways, relatively. We may wind up looking for any planet we can live on, welcome or not, and trying to land this ship manually." He looked at Vince with what seemed genuine regret. "I hope not—I've been thinking, the last few hours, that the best thing for us would be to fall into the hands of the Lenj. I am embarrassed to mention this, Kul Lo, but the medicine you need to keep your eyesight is back on Shann, if it has not been destroyed in the invasion! I am hoping we find the Lenj, and that they can supply the treatment you need."

Vince sat down again and tried not to clench his fists. He glared at the Onsian. "Oh, fine, fine! Well, when I go blind you can lead me around. Just give me a grip on that air hose of yours, and—"

Gondal waved a tentacle. "Do not embrace despair so lustfully! You will be all right for several hundred hours yet, I think. And I cannot believe this will be a long journey. The Lenj, to have traveled from cell to cell, must have possessed speed incomparably faster than our own FTL. I feel confident that just a few hours—"

Vince got up and turned his back on the Onsian. "Oh, well, all right then. Let me know if you begin to feel any less confident." He strode to the forward hatch of the segment and stepped through it. Behind him, he heard Gondal's hissing chuckle.

Akorra, when she was awake and fairly clear of mind, revealed an odd mixture of knowledge and ignorance about the Lenjan ship.

"We know," she said, sipping a glass of some juice freshly thawed from its ages-long storage, "that this class of ship was the smallest of three sizes of nonmilitary transport. They traveled from cell to cell, apparently for ordinary commerce as well as official business."

Gondal asked, "In what part of the empire was our own cell?"

She turned her pale eyes upon the Onsian. "There was no hint of that. They were so painstaking to conceal where they'd gone—"

Gondal waved a tentacle impatiently. "All right, we may learn more firsthand. How is this ship powered? I understand you are a physicist."

Akorra blinked a smile. "Only marginally. We know that their usual power for ships was immensely more efficient than the coins using the simple hydrogen fusion. No one has made even a tempting guess as to its nature, except that it must release, controllably, the most basic energy of matter."

"Well," Gondal asked, with a glance at Vince, "certainly they traveled fast, did they not?"

She looked faintly astonished. "Of course." She turned to Vince. "I am not familiar with your species. Is your science more advanced than that of Ness?"

Vince gave Gondal a sour look. "No. The fact is . . . I suppose there's no sense in holding back the truth now. My race hadn't even developed an FTL drive when Ness found us. Part of the reason I'm here is that my world is on the edge of the Chullwei sector, and the Nesse feared. . . . You understand, we may be, uh, primitive by your standards, but we can learn. And there are a fair number of us, and we have resources."

Gondal hissed in amusement. "No wonder you were such a tyro when the Nesse delivered you to me! Well, you must admit this, Kul Lo, though I have been over-handed with you, you have seen a great deal for a primitive!"

Vince felt his face go hot. "I've seen things I'd just as soon have passed up, and I'm looking at one of them now." He faced Akorra. "What do you think of this 'Wolami' we seem to be headed for? Was it some center of Lenjan civilization? Or a military base? Or what?"

She eyed him, curiosity on her delicately furred face. "I do not know. I had heard the quotation about Wolami girding for battle, but I assumed it was only myth. The Lenj did have those, you know." She glanced at Gondal. "Have you been all over this ship?"

"Only superficially. Each segment seems equipped to translocate separately, if need be. Computers and power sources are well buried in the spaces between living quarters and the outer hull—and there is no access, which speaks for the reliability of Lenjan apparatus! The computers of all segments seem to be linked now—at least, the keyboards are. There are viewers, of course, but they are blank." He paused. "There are suits, and parts of suits, aboard. If I can assemble something that will fit me, and if we are en route long enough, I may go outside and see what sort of non-space or non-time we are traveling in. However, I do not think that a great deal of time will elapse."

He was right. Only a few more hours passed, and Akorra's study of the ship had barely begun, when the ubiquitous mechanical voice said, "Attention. Wolami is within instrument range. The power sources of the receiving depot there have been heavily drained. This ship can pinpoint to arrival on its own power, and as there are no indications of damage or obstruction on Wolami, that will be done unless override instructions are given."

Vince, staring helplessly at the ceiling from which the voice came, was aware of Gondal's sibilant cursing in the next segment. So far, neither the Onsian nor Akorra had made the smallest advance toward learning how to "instruct" the ship's computers, though the keyboards were standard enough. Vince stepped to the hatch and exchanged glances with Gondal. The Onsian gestured to him. "If you have any gods, Vinz Kul Lo, I suggest you pray to them!"

"Yeah," Vince muttered, "if I have any. Especially wherever we are now."

After the matter-of-fact voice announced that the ship was safely in a cage on Wolami, there was a period of silence in which Vince, Gondal, and Akorra sat looking at each other. Geegee stood to one side, grinning.

Gondal was the first to speak. "No doubt there are external sensors to tell us whether we are in breathable air, or in some corrosive atmosphere, or in none at all. But as we have not mastered whatever devilish mathematics the Lenj built into their computers, and as it is not reasonable to expect that we *can* master it within the next few minutes, I propose the simplest of tests: let us crack one of the end hatches the barest trifle, and see what happens. At least, we understand the manual lock-controls." He turned both heads toward Vince. "You say even you can see no images on the viewers?"

Vince shook his head. "Even if we're in a chamber that glows like the one we left, the sensors would be too feeble to register it. I mean, *it* would be too feeble to . . ."

The Onsian sighed. "All right, since I have my cannister (which is going to need pumping up before long, if I can find the right gasses aboard), *I* will make the test. You may close the inner hatch behnd me if you wish; though I will be very crowded in the lock."

Vince looked around at the others. "Akorra had better go into the next compartment. I'll stay here in case you need help." He glanced at Geegee, who curled hearing-organs in agreement.

They got the inner hatch open and stood by while Gondal shaped himself into the meager space. Neither Vince nor Geegee moved to close the inner hatch, and Gondal didn't insist. Vince couldn't help grinning at the Onsian's efforts to coil his breathing-appendage and attach it to his cannister. He watched as tentacles writhed forward and fumbled at the outer hatch's manual controls. An amber light flashed on, there was a scraping sound, and the outer hatch began to slide open. There was a faint hiss of escaping air. Vince went tenser, but the sound dwindled quickly, to be replaced by a not-dissimilar sound from Gondal. "The pressure is lower outside—but not by as much as 10 percent, I think. I am going to inhale cautiously from the crack." The hose-like member worked itself forward.

Gondal sighed, reached for the controls, and opened the hatch completely. "Nothing wrong with the air that a small addition of ammonia would not cure!"

Vince, peering past the Onsian's bulk, felt relief pierce him like an arrow. "I can see! It's—it's a chamber of some sort, all right! There's a smooth wall opposite, and it glows like the one we left!"

Vince, doing the reconnoitering, had to stand in the darkness of the chamber for several minutes before he was sure that the glow here was slightly weaker than the one on Shann.

There was a silence here—such a silence that he instinctively felt, rightly or wrongly, that the place had been deserted for eons.

The five enormous translocation-cages, other than the one that held the newly arrived ship, were empty. Aside from those, the chamber was strikingly bare, with no cell-map mockup, no globe representing a world, no banks of dials (except the ones on the individual control-panels of the cages). None of the strange apparatus that had made his nerves twinge on Shann. The only thing here, in fact, other than the cages, was an assembly of big locker-like things, a row on row of them with aisles between, in one end of the chamber. They might, he thought, be food storage lockers, tool bins, and such.

From where he stood, just outside the cage, he could see three tunnels leading out of the chamber; and from the arrangement, he suspected there might be a fourth hidden by the lockers.

He turned back toward the ship, from which Gondal's snakeheads poked impatiently. "Come on out with flashlights, if you want to."

In the next half hour, they had the immediate area of the chamber thoroughly explored.

The tunnel in the wall opposite the cages led to a smaller chamber on the same level and fifty yards away, protected by double turns in the tunnel. A second tunnel, the one Vince had rightly guessed at, ended in another smaller chamber. Both those lesser spaces were dead ends, except for ventilation shafts a foot in diameter, and were empty. A few faint smudges on walls and floors hinted that there'd been something installed temporarily at one time, such as bunks and partitions. A third tunnel, in the long bare wall opposite the cages, branched only into a series of ventilation ducts.

The fourth tunnel, after initial turns, showed promise. But it did not climb or descend; it stretched on into, for all Vince could tell, solid rock. Vince, Geegee, and two of the latter's warriors started out to explore that.

Vince was carrying the flashlight. Five hundred yards or so along, Geegee, just behind him, said, "There is a faint draft from ahead, Vinz Kul Lo. Can you feel it?"

"No, I can't. Is it warmer or cooler?"

"Warmer. Is that significant?"

Vince sighed. "I don't know. It's possible, though, that it means radioactivity. I'll tell you what—Why don't we turn off the light and go on slowly? If there's radioactivity, I'll be able to see it, or see something excited by it. I—it occurs to me that this tunnel might lead to a power installation. I hope not. At least one tunnel ought to lead to open air!"

"Should according to *our* feelings, Vinz. Neither you nor I feel comfortable enclosed. But suppose the Lenj had no need or desire to reach open air, except as ventilation? Suppose they arrived and departed here only by ship?" He paused. "However, a thought occurs to me: perhaps we *are* headed toward open air, and the temperature is higher than in here. Possibly unbearably high."

Vince led on, pondering Geegee's remark. After awhile he said, "Well, anyway, the glow's not getting any stronger."

"That is good, friend Vinz. Shall we proceed without the light?"

Vince hesitated. "Do you mind? I—my special ability in the dark gives me confidence. For instance, I could see a dangerous beast before it saw us!"

Geegee chuckled. "A good point, and one which you once demonstrated to me! Lead, then."

Vince went on. The tunnel ran straight and unblemished by cracks or seepage. Here and there small ventilation ducts led out of it, but those must be well protected too.

Eventually he saw what appeared to be an end. "I think there's a right-angle turn ahead. Why don't you wait here while I reconnoiter?"

He moved on slowly, a little excited. A turn meant at least another chamber. He was almost sure he, too, could feel the greater warmth of the air now.

Presently he stood peering down a short stretch of tunnel. He turned and called to Geegee, "Come on! There's daylight just ahead!"

He didn't realize, until he himself had started to trot, that he wasn't being very prudent. But he met no trouble.

Just seeing daylight was an immense relief, though he felt a leaden uneasiness at the obvious alienness of this world. Shann, by the diffuse light of the stars, hadn't seemed so terribly strange, there'd been seas and mountains and the thick vegetation. He'd been able to *feel* it was familiar. But this world, in his deepest level of awareness, could not be any region of Earth.

The tunnel opened onto the steep, though not vertical, face of a cliff. The rock was a weathered medium-gray—*greenish*-gray, which was part of the alienness. Below, the cliff fell away a mile or more to a pale, ribbed desert that stretched to a horizon lost in heat-shimmer. This face of the cliff was in shadow, a long slanting shadow that reached out miles across the bleached, barren flat; but still the air was warm enough to make him perspire. The perspiration, he noted, dried fast. And quickly, breathing that dry, tepid air, his mouth and nostrils were dry.

A world in which one had better carry plenty of water.

Geegee, looking over his shoulder, muttered, "That entire expanse—it looks like the sand on the beaches of my world!"

Vince nodded. "It's sand, all right—the floor of what once was an ocean. Sand—and salt, maybe." The dune-rippled expanse showed various tints of bleached olive-green, somehow queasily strange. He wondered if, on this world, the iron he thought of as normal was replaced by some other element—chromium, for instance.

As for vegetation, there was, surprisingly, a little. The bleached-olive, billowing line that wound off into the desert must be a thicket of trees along some gully. Near him, where soil had lodged in hollows of the crumbling rock, spikelike grass, the same color as the distant trees, grew sparsely.

He leaned out to see the source of the gully. It must leave some part of the cliff a mile or more to his left, behind a bulge of rock. There might, he realized, be an ancient canyon there. For this cliff-face had once known the rough caress of surf (he could see other caves on a level with this one). And where there'd been seas, there'd been rain and run-off and canyons. It was hard to imagine rain here now, but possibly, somewhere inland, mountains did extract some moisture from the wind. And there might be a shrunken sea beyond the horizon.

The thought made him feel even drier, and he reached for the flask he'd brought, uncapped it, and took a swallow. "I suppose we can climb down this cliff if there's ever any need to. But we've plenty of packaged food in the ship. Anyway, I wouldn't expect much live game here, would you?"

Geegee chuckled softly. "I would not expect it, no. But observe—at the base of this cliff, where it is visible a little to our left—Is not that a trail in the sand?"

Vince peered in the indicated direction. The faint line, in the deepest part of the cliff's shadow, wasn't at all obvious. But it *did* look like a game-trail! And it must be regularly used, else sand would drift over it!

He felt a now-familiar prickling move up his spine. "I suppose we ought to report it to the rest!"

Geegee turned and muttered to one of his warriors, who disappeared into the tunnel.

Vince found a level spot and sat down, leaning back against the rock. He took time to look around the cave into which the tunnel opened. It wasn't more than twenty feet deep, and fairly high-vaulted, so it was light; still, the tunnel-mouth wouldn't be distinguishable from out on the desert, nor from any extreme angle to the sides. "I wonder if the Lenj considered this a secret outlet. In any case, I don't think I'll be climbing down this cliff for a while."

Geegee curled a hearing-organ. "Nor I. How, friend Vinz, could a sea vanish like this?"

Vince shrugged. "The climate got warmer, maybe. Or, for all I know, the Lenj may have used up the water. That would be as plausible a starting-point for their energy as any, I suppose." He let his eyes rove along the cliff.

Suddenly he came to his feet. "There—a bird of some kind!"

Geegee blinked at him in surprise. "Had you not seen them before? Your eyes, then, are not exceptional in day-light! I have watched a dozen or more in the last few minutes. They have aeries in the cliff-caves on that bulge. They fly more ponderously than the birds of Shann—after all, the air is a little thinner here—but I saw at least two mounting with small game in their talons. They swoop down in the direction of that waterway, fly up and down it, pounce, and return with their prey. It is a thing that makes me feel less far from home."

Vince considered. "I guess I feel the same." He got another mouthful of water, swirled it around and swal-lowed. "Those birds have a wingspread of six feet or more. I guess they need it. What about your eyes, Geegee? Aren't you dazzled here?"

"No, and I am surprised at that. I presume my pupils are mere lines now—is that so?"

"Yes."

"Nevertheless I do not feel uncomfortable—not yet, at least. On Shann there is lightning, you know; perhaps the eyes of my species are adapted to tolerate that. But what a treasure your night-vision would be among us!" He appeared to muse for a while. "What of your own world, Vinz? Is it beautiful like Shann? Or like—Yes, this Wolami has a beauty too, does it not? A grandeur? To be able to see so far, and so clearly. . . . Tell me of your own world."

Vince felt a sudden tightness in his throat. He turned his face from the ipsisumoedan. "It's not too unlike Shann, except for our sun. We have trees and oceans and moun-tains. And a wide variety of animal life. Some parts of it are almost like this, in a way—we call them "deserts"— But the shades there are brownish, not greenish. The crust of my world has shifted much in the past, and what were former ocean floors are now dry." He paused for a minute. "There are places on my world where water is frozen solid. You've never seen that, I suppose."

"No. What is it like?"

"Like glass, sometimes. That is, like the material the Vred use for windows in their shuttleboats. But much more brittle. And sometimes it falls from the clouds in a form like—well, like a very fluffy kind of fur, pure white, although that's not a good analogy."

Geegee breathed softly. "Is a sun, as I have been told, really a star around which a world revolves?"

"Yes. And there may be more than one world revolving about a star, at various distances. Quite a few stars have at least one planet. That's why there are so many species who've learned to travel in space."

"A thrilling thing. But tell me, Vinz Kul Lo, since your world has a sun, like Wolami, is your sky such a marvelous color as this? Such a pure, glowing shade of blue?"

Vince waited until he could control his voice. "Yes, our sky is just as blue. When it's clear, it's just as blue."

Wolami's sky purpled as the hidden sun fell farther into what Vince now recognized as the west. The shadow of the cliff stretched out until it engulfed the whole desert except for a vague streak of still-dazzling sand at the limit of seeing. The aerie-dwelling birds accelerated their efforts as if anxious to hoard up prey before night. Or maybe it was just that the small ground animals were more active now that the air was cooler. Vince could definitely feel that welcome drop in temperature; perhaps, he thought, this planet's atmosphere was enough thinner than Earth's so that the day's heat radiated away significantly faster. He did see one animal loping across the sand; at least collie-sized or he couldn't have seen it from here. It had short hind legs but longer front ones. It traveled in a peculiar lope that put all four feet off the ground at once—more of a series of bounds, actually, an eerily strange gait. Possibly that was necessary because of its long body that had to be kept bowed up in the middle. He couldn't see whether it had a tail, ears, or snout. It emerged from the dusty-pale tree thicket along the waterway as if startled by something, ran downstream, then reentered the thicket.

It was a little while later that Vince saw the file of bipeds trotting along the trail at the cliff's base.

They were like caricatures of humans—or possibly of some other anthropoids, for their faces suggested baboon masks. Their gray-brown fur was sparse and short, as might be expected on a hot world. Torsos and arms were elongated, though not apelike, while their legs were almost ludicrously short. They moved in a steady trot which, he realized, might be a normal walk for them. Their garments consisted of colorful loose cloaks that came to their knees. He strained his eyes to see why the cloaks billowed so oddly, and finally decided that they were made of strips sewn together at shoulder, waist, and hem—strips of cloth, bright-green and white and tan. Each individual carried a short spear, plus a small bundle of some kind at the small of his back, and (though Geegee had to tell him this) knife scabbards attached to the cloaks at the waist, without belts.

Despite the spears, Vince didn't find the half-dozen beings threatening. They trotted serenely, their attention obviously casual. "A hunting party?" he suggested.

Geegee flicked an ear-tentacle in the equivalent of a shrug. "Perhaps. If so, they are on their way out, to hunt in the twilight, for they carry no game. And is it not doubtful that they would be moving *away* from that wooded gully? I see no other likely source of water, so I assume tentatively that they live there. Rather, I would guess, a reconnoitering-party." He turned and grinned at Vince.

Vince wondered about the grin. "You're probably a better judge of that than I, but is there some special reason you think so?"

"A special reason indeed. Follow the line of that gully away from the cliff for perhaps half a mile. At about the point where the four-legged beast was flushed awhile ago. Do you not see a similar party?"

Vince squinted, running his eyes along the line of trees. Finally he made out the group, tiny with distance. They seemed to wear cloaks identical with those of the nearer sextet (which by now was around a bulge of the cliff, out of sight). Something about the way they stood made Vince's pulse stir a little faster. "Do you get the impression . . . well, that they're staring up at us?"

"I do," Geegee said. "I would offer odds on it. Of course, we do not know how good their eyes are; nor can we be sure there is not something else on the cliff near us that they are staring at. But there are common patterns of behavior in most animal life, are there not? That group acts as if they'd seen us here, and were astounded if not dismayed!"

Vince, a chill moving up his spine, found his hand straying to the Lenjan energy-pistol at his waist. "Damn it! Now I won't feel comfortable whether I'm sitting here on watch, or inside where I can't see! I can't tell whether they have spears like the other six or not. Can you?"

"They have. But they do not grasp them, I think, in a way that suggests hostility. I am wondering whether they think we are gods. There may be legends of the time when the Lenj were here."

Vince pondered that. "Then you don't assume *they* are degenerate descendants of the Lenj?"

"Hardly, friend Vinz. These are smaller and slighter even than Akorra. Whereas the Lenj built their ships, I think, for somewhat larger bipeds."

Vince sighed. "That's true." He'd been thinking about his eyes, and the possible help the Lenj might give. "Well, we'll just have to be watchful. Especially at night."

Geegee chuckled. "I'll put even *my* eyes against theirs at night here, Vinz—if the stars are not feebler than those of Shann. While you . . ."

Vince shrugged. "Suppose we stay here awhile, and watch?"

"A sound thought." Geegee turned to his remaining warrior and said something in the ipsisumoedan language. The warrior left to report. Vince turned his attention to the sextet of natives near the waterway.

For a few minutes longer the distant group stayed where they were. Then, casting frequent glances toward the cave (or so Vince thought), they began to trot up-gully, in a file like the other bunch. He supposed they could no longer see him in what was by now full dusk. Finally, hurrying, they vanished beyond the cliffs.

He stared around nervously for a few minutes more, saw no sign of stealthy approach up the cliff, and turned his attention to the stars. They seemed very feeble and few.

He sat wondering glumly whether the stars were indeed dimmer here, or whether his eyes were already failing. The stars became no brighter as time went by. Then, as the last purpleness of the sky turned to black, he became aware of a diffuse glow, barely above the northeastern horizon.

He stared at that, the dull lump in his stomach getting worse. In that glow he could make out dimensionless points of light, and dark areas, and—yes, there was no doubt about it—a tendency toward arrangement in spiral bands. He breathed deeply of the now-cool air. "Geegee, unless I'm wrong, I'm looking at one edge of a galaxy. Can you see that glow?"

"Dimly, I can see it."

"It's . . . I don't like the thought, but my guess is, that's *our* galaxy! If it is, we've come a distance I don't like to try to calculate!"

The ipsisumoedan chuckled. "I grasp the thought. But to me there is little difference. Whether we traveled from Shann to the nearest star, or beyond the farthest star, it is still a journey I will never retrace on my own two feet!"

Vince brooded over that for a minute. "No. Nor I on mine."

A hundred hours had passed since the first trip out to the tunnel exit. With familiarity, the way became short and routine. Now there were always at least two of Gee-gee's warriors on watch there, and Vince and Gondal had finished stringing a telephone line along the tunnel so communication would be constant. The general rule for anyone visiting the cave during the daytime was to keep far enough back to be invisible to any natives staring up from the desert floor. Each member of the party had been out to view the desert at least once.

Just now, Vince was inside, pondering something. He looked up at Gondal, patiently poring over a bit of Lenjan equipment, then instead reached for the newly installed telephone. "Geegee?"

From the tunnel exit, the ipsisumoedan answered, "Yes, friend Vinz."

"Is it fully dark out there now?"

"I think so. I can see no purple in the sky."

"Can you see that diffused glow? The one I thought was our galaxy?"

"I see it."

"Good. I was beginning to wonder if I'd lost my mind and imagined it! Is it in the same position?"

"Precisely the same, Vinz."

Vince sighed. "And how about the stars? Have you gotten to know any patterns yet?"

"There are so few stars, I hesitate to speak of patterns. But such stars as I recognize are in the same places. Is that what you want to know?"

"Yes. Thanks, Geegee." Vince looked up to meet the paired eyes of Gondal, who'd stopped to listen. "There's something I don't understand. Each time I've been out at night the stars and that—that glow have been in the same places. Yet the apparent movement of the sun proves that Wolami has a rotation!"

From the telephone came Geegee's deep chuckle. "Perhaps you are thinking too much of your own world, Vinz, and the conditions that exist there. To me, Wolami's circumstances are more clear. Shann has a rotation, and the stars appear to move accordingly. Wolami is without rotation. And what you call the sun here is *not* a star around which Wolami revolves. It is like one of Shann's moons, comparatively close, revolving around Wolami."

Vince drew in his breath sharply, stared at the telephone, and stared at Gondal. He felt his face grow hot. Into the phone he said, "I—I'll talk to you later. It sounds as if you're right!"

Slowly, he walked over to the Onsian. "A sun revolving around a world . . . Have you ever encountered, anywhere in the cell, a—a moon that emitted light? *Intense* light?"

Gondal waved a tentacle. "If you are not obstinate about what you call a moon—Certainly. I can think of a dozen worlds that have put light-sources into orbit to supplement their suns. I know of one—I would not be greeted cordially were I to return there—that, lacking a sun, was made to bloom by installing powerful illuminators on the closest of its moons. What is so surprising about that?"

Vince stared dazedly at Gondal, then at Akorra, who'd just come out of the Lenjan ship. "The legend . . . 'Wolami lazes beneath his lamp' . . . The gods! The, uh, sun here rises once in a little over thirty hours. It's—it's a satellite! And that spiral nebula—that *is* our galaxy!"

Akorra came nearer, excitement on her delicately furred face. "Then we *did* leave our local cell! Oh, I wish I'd had time to study that three-dimensional map before we left!"

Gondal said, "Hiss-hiss-hiss. No doubt that was one of the projects Zarpi had in mind for you. He'd heard, somehow, some ancient tale. . . . But here, in these computers we're struggling with, the same information is surely locked up. If we can master that insane mathematics . . ."

Vince said, "I'll put my hopes of ever getting back to Shann in that programming-disc that brought us here. Any progress with that, Akorra?"

The female Nessen looked at him with something like

compassion clouding her delicate face. "No real progress, Vinz. It, too, involves the incomprehensible mathematics. I know only this so far: the program is still inside the disc, and also in the ship's computers. Once the mathematics is clear, I hope we can tease the program out and reverse it."

Vinz turned away. "Yes. Well, I'm certainly no mathematician. I think I'll go out and have another look at the sky."

CHAPTER SEVENTEEN

ZARPI, concealing the rage that was a constant fever in his blood now, stood waiting for Shkzak, Commander of the Chullwei invasion forces, to speak. He must not, he'd decided, let his erstwhile ally guess at the recent debacle here inside the mountain.

Shkzak's tiny eyes flickered over the long bank of machinery, pausing upon each raw scar where the rupter-beam had slashed. "You were clumsy indeed to stage a battle here! Could you not have taken the place with more finesse?"

Zarpi held his face immobile. "Perhaps I have not your talent for treachery. Negotiations with the Vred making a last stand here, were going very well; they showed no suspicion. But the gas we were pumping in must have left a few of them conscious, to do this damage in pure spite."

The rough-furred Chullwei opened his mouth in what might be, to its perpetrator, a grin, but which looked simply like a display of fangs. "Your reference to treachery is amusing. Did you really expect us to be so obtuse as to let you outwit us? I simply took precautions against that. So far as the Vred treasury is concerned, I will hold to our original agreement—you may keep half. I am not concerned with trifles. We had intelligence of Lenjan installations on Shann, and I merely let you think you were cozening me so you would lead us to the planet." Shkzak turned and ambled toward the great elongated cluster of translucent hexahedrons, across which the rupter had slashed, leaving fused severed ends of wire and a few crumpled hexahedrons. "No basic damage, I think—the secrets will be in the computers connected to this mockup. Probably, in any case, this is only an indicator-map upon which various things were reported." He half-turned and peered down the row of translocation cages. "*There* is the real treasure—the ancient empire's means of travel! You are certain the Vred have not solved it?"

Zarpi thought carefully about his answer. Shkzak's offhand manner didn't disarm him—the Chullwei Task Force Commander would be alert for any inconsistency. "The Vred, I am certain, never even suspected that this chamber was here. It was not until my own men bored a way up to it that the band of die-hards took refuge here. I started to explain, but you. . . . The crew I had at work was not numerous, and Vred from a secret hideout were able to overrun them. Thereafter I felt compelled to pursue them more discreetly. But they simply rode the elevator up—Marvelous, is it not that it should still operate after so many thousands of years?—and hid themselves in this chamber."

Shkzak flicked him an apparently casual glance. "So you had no more than your original suspicion of what might be here? Well, despite your expected attempt at trickery, and a little clumsiness in allowing this superficial damage, things have not turned out badly! I shall shortly feel able to dispatch a ship home with news that will astound certain of my superiors—may their skeptical, supercilious faces rot. Where do those tunnels lead?"

Zarpi smiled what he hoped was a disarming smile to cover his uncertainty. There'd been no time, since the incredible whisking away of Akorra, to explore, hardly time even to collect his wits, before the Chullwei were down and swarming over the place. "I have no idea. It took us an hour to pump fresh air into here after we gassed the Vred, and a dangerous amount still lingers in the tunnels. Unfortunately all our gas masks were inaccessible due to a mishap. . . . At least one tunnel, I suspect, may lead to the surface, for there is a small discrepancy in the number of Vred bodies we found. A very few of the die-hards

142

may have escaped to the surface, or may still be lurking in tunnels."

The Chullwei commander waved a paw-like hand carelessly. "We'll root them out, if they are. Now, Zarpi, I suggest you have what's left of your crews begin removing the loot you want. I intend to fortify this mountain thoroughly, and booby-trap it as well, so that I can blow it to dust instantly from a safe distance if anything threatening ever comes from the-gods-know-where while our scientists are studying the apparatus. Non-Chullwei will be unwelcome—except that I will require you, individually, to remain here for a time. Your crews will remain at the colony meanwhile."

Zarpi hoped his murderous, frustrated anger didn't show in his face. "Well . . . I had aspired highly; but after all I am only a minor entrepreneur and this operation has been profitable. I, ah, have not heard what status you have imposed upon other guests of the colony."

Shkzak showed his fangs, as if he understood some of Zarpi's indirection. "We are going to let the Vred continue to manage things temporarily, under a close watch of course. Guests, we may allow to leave after we have sufficiently secured the vicinity of Shann. We have no need to liquidate such an array of pirates—some of them, indeed, may be useful to us. We are even letting the Vred keep the half of their treasury you do not take. Their home world is not powerful, but we'd just as soon not antagonize it unnecessarily."

This time Zarpi was able to smile with something of sincerity. He hadn't come off so badly in this first confrontation with the commander of the powerful Task Force. He hadn't revealed anything about Akorra or the missing Lenjan-disc artifact, which, if he could recover it, might still yield secrets of immense value. And he hadn't revealed that the natives here, the ipsisumoedans, had somehow penetrated the mountain; there's been time, at least, to police up the chamber a little.

What did bother him, what he needed time to think about, was who else, other than the natives, had been

143

involved in the bewildering episode. There'd definitely been one beam from a handgun—a type none of his men carried. And his flashlight had paused, just before things erupted, upon what was certainly the end of a ship, nestled in one of the huge cages.

Time might solve some of the mysteries. Of one thing he felt reasonably sure: if some other guest or guests had ambushed him here in the chamber, using the natives as allies, and had departed in a Lenjan ship, then absences from the colony's guest list would reveal who. It pleased him, under the circumstances, that a temporary quarantine existed, and that he himself did not have to leave.

But the departure of that Lenjan ship (which, he hoped fervently, the Chullwei would never learn about) threatened trouble. Suppose Akorra, with some other pirate and a group of natives, returned voluntarily or otherwise. The Chullwei might question her. Or they might destroy the ship the instant it reappeared. He'd have to make schemes to dupe Shkzak somehow, though the commander would certainly be watching him very closely.

He made a gesture at the big furry being, then turned and walked toward the elevator column. A Chullwei soldier with a heavy gun eyed him contemptuously, but stood aside. What Zarpi needed first of all, once he got the loot aboard his ships and got back to the field, was some food and a prudent draught of whisky, and a chance to lie down and rest and think. Future events might be sudden and unpredictable, but he intended to be as ready as possible to meet them.

CHAPTER EIGHTEEN

Wolami's night sky hadn't changed.

Geegee seemed to be allowing Vince time to ponder. Then, finally, the big humanoid asked softly, "Will you explain some things to me, Vinz? What little my people have learned from the Vred does not equip me to understand."

"Of course. What puzzles you?"

"This concept of a vast artificial light moving around Wolami, for one thing. I understand more or less how Shann's moons revolve slowly about her, with the pull of gravity balancing their tendency to move away, though I have trouble seeing how such a balance could be stable over a long time. But this satellite here moves much faster. Why is that?"

"Because it's much closer."

Geegee seemed to mull that over. "If I tie a weight on a cord and whirl it around my head, I can demonstrate centrifugal force. But the faster I whirl it, the more it struggles to move away. How is it, then, that a satellite of a world is closer when it travels faster?"

Vince sighed. How he wished the theory could be put as simply as he'd first learned it, without the complications of possible artificial gravity, linear motion of the primary, and such. "Well . . . the gravity of any body grows weaker the farther you are from it. So a more distant satellite, such as Shann's moons, has only to tug against a weak pull. Therefore, the centrifugal force of its revolution need not be great. Actually, the distance of a satellite is determined by its speed in orbit and by the strength of the primary's gravity. If the gravity is weak or the satellite's speed is high, the satellite orbits far out. I mean . . . well, can you see the relationship between orbit, speed, and gravity?"

Geegee chuckled softly. "Vaguely, though it makes my logic-cog ache. Then a satellite is confined forever in a specific orbit, depending upon its speed and the gravity that holds it?"

"Well, uh, no. I suppose it would be, theoretically, if it traveled in a perfect circle and there were nothing to slow it down or speed it up, or pull it out of orbit. But most orbits are not perfect circles. Some are very eccentric, so elongated that the satellite loops far out and returns only once in a long time. And while it's far away, moving slowly and feeling only a weak tug of gravity, things may happen to change its orbit. Such as the pull of other bodies, even distant stars. Then there are other complications. While it's close, there may be enough atmosphere for it to pass through to slow it down. I—the truth is, Geegee, that I've never been entirely convinced by the theory myself! Suppose, for instance, that the primary is moving very fast, and not necessarily in a straight line. *It* may be in orbit around something else. Also, while a satellite in a long elliptical orbit is on the far leg, why does it act as if it were being attracted *not* to where its primary is at the moment, but *where the primary will be when the satellite gets back?*"

"Are you asking *me,* friend Vinz?"

Vince laughed. "I'm asking questions I didn't have the nerve to ask when I was being taught. Oh, the theory is that satellite and primary have a common linear motion so that they act as if the primary were at a standstill. But I suspect that the truth is this: there's no such thing as a stable orbit actually; some only seem stable by time-standards of ordinary living beings. Over very long periods, even tiny events must change an orbit."

Geegee said, "But this light-giving satellite here has been in orbit a very long time."

"Compared to my lifetime or yours, yes. On a cosmic time-scale, no. In any case, being a Lenjan artifact, it may have regulatory appartus."

"That, Vinz, is another thing I have been wondering about. Is it merely long-lived, or is it self-regulatory, or do the Lenj return periodically to adjust it? I am not content to sit here in this cave until I die of old age. Nor do I think well of simply going back to Shann via the same transportation that brought us—assuming that Gondal and Akorra can achieve even that much. It would comfort me to hope that the Lenj are *not* extinct, and this place not completely forgotten." Geegee paused. "Another question, if you will: I assume from your explanation that this artificial sun is beyond what atmosphere Wolami has. How far?"

"Hm. That's a good question. I'd have to know certain things, and calculate. But let's say, somewhere in the vicinity of twenty-five thousand miles." He mused. "If it's a simple unforced orbit."

Geegee grunted. "Not far, if we could devise some kind of ship to take us above the atmosphere."

"No, but I imagine the heat would be more than we'd like—unless it's all directed down, with the far side dark. What do you have in mind? What good would it do us to reach it, anyway?"

"I was thinking of the legend you quoted: 'When the lamp is extinguished, then will Wolami gird for battle.' It does not take much imagination to interpret that as meaning, if the lamp goes out, its builders will come to see what is wrong."

"Oh!" Vince felt blood rush to his face. Why the devil was he so slow in thinking of such things himself?

"Another thought," Geegee said. "If Wolami is a sphere, and the satellite moves around it in an orbit which is not far from a circle, and the ground does not rotate under it in any way, then two points on Wolami, opposite each other, will get almost no light at all."

Vince sighed. "You're right of course, they'd correspond to the poles of a normal planet. But a satellite, deliberately placed to warm and light a world, might be programmed—if it had a drive of some sort—to precess around in its orbit. Then there'd be seasons. And even if there *were* north and south 'poles' here, what use would they be to us?"

"I cannot imagine, friend Vinz. But any such things might be useful in some way—to attract the Lenj, for instance, if the Lenj still exist. So long as I am sitting here, I may as well be thinking. And that brings up another subject."

"What?"

"We have seen so little of Wolami. Dare we not explore a bit? At least we could climb to the top of this cliff; see what the country is like above it, and get a wider view of the desert. There could even be Lenj ruins, in which we might find knowledge we need. Tomorrow, if I can get the agreement of the rest of you, I will take a pair of my warriors and climb up."

Vince got restlessly to his feet. "You could be speaking my thoughts, Geegee. You have *my* vote,—and unless someone ties me down, I'm going along!"

Wolami's morning sun was hot on Vince's back, though he was wearing a wide-brimmed, makeshift hat and the coolest garments he could find. He hauled himself up the last steep twenty feet of weathered cliff and stood beside Geegee on the rim. He worked his shoulders uneasily, wondering if the intense light were dangerous. Gondal and Akorra hadn't yet got around to rigging up some kind of radiation detector.

The two warriors finished the climb and stood with them, squinting curiously at the low, almost bare ridge that hid the country inland. Vince turned and stared out over the desert. The line of trees marking the waterway (or gully) was hardly more than a chalk-scribe from this height; not could he see anything on the horizon—there was just the heat-shimmer. No clouds, no haze, except what might be a low dust-storm to the southeast, marred the baking sky.

He turned to Geegee. "I suppose we ought to get onto that ridge, then go along it and try to find the source of that waterway."

Geegee flicked a hearing-organ and led off.

It took half an hour to top the ridge. Vince, with something like a tide of relief, stood staring westward. Now there was evidence of water!

The mountain peaks couldn't be over twenty miles away, rising abruptly beyond a valley as flat and bleached as the desert a mile below. They were gnarled old peaks, with signs of ancient glacier-sculptoring subsequently softened by erosion. A few slopes boasted grassfields of the bleached olive-green color.

But what brought relief flooding over Vince was the presence, on the flanks of the highest peaks, of dazzling-white patches. He turned, grinning, to the ipsisumoedans. "That's what I was telling you about—snow!"

Geegee stared at the phenomenon for several minutes before speaking. "You say it is frozen—with this heat pouring down upon it?"

Vince told him, "It's no doubt melting steadily. But at that altitude it can last quite a while. It may have been half a year since it fell there—and by the way, it implies seasons! So that artificial sun *does* precess, or something. I feel a few thousand light-years nearer home now!"

Geegee chuckled. "Let us hope the natives here do not reverse your feeling. Have you noted the trail along the top of this ridge?"

Vince blinked at him, glanced down, and instinctively felt for the Lenjan handgun he'd brought. The trail was faint, but detectable—more a matter of stones being absent than any worn path. He looked around. Anything that saw them on the ridge would have to climb bare slopes to reach them.

Geegee was already leading northward.

It was when they were close enough to see the great canyon ahead that the natives came solemnly to meet them.

The spears that had been almost invisible at a distance

looked formidable close up. They were metal-tipped and metal-shafted, and there was no sign of rust. Besides the spears, each of the six natives carried, in a scabbard at the reinforced waistline of his odd cloak of ribbons, a knife.

If there was any intent to use the weapons, the natives hid it well. They came on single-file, in their odd little quick-step, solemn and silent. Vince saw that his first long-range impression had been fairly accurate: they were slender, sparsely covered with dark fur over gray skins, and did have faces suggesting baboons. But the skulls were human-size, and the small eyes looked intelligent. They weren't much over five feet tall, though they'd be considerably taller with human legs.

At twenty-five yards he could detect the awe that gripped them. They stopped fifteen yards away, all of them, after a look around, dropping their spears to the baked soil.

The leader, wrinkled and with half an ear missing, came slowly forward with a slight limp, stopped, and made a half bow. There was deference, rather than fear, in his manner. And then he spoke in perfect Lenjan, as Vince's jaw dropped. "I am Shontemur, Chief of twenty twenties. Are you the Great Ones?"

Vince stood paralyzed until he realized with a start that he was supposed to be the civilized member of his party. He swallowed to get his voice working. "We are, uh, not Lenj. Is that what you mean?" Immediately he realized it was a foolish admission. He flushed, but it was too late.

But Shontemur sagged in obvious disappointment. "We were not sure. The Great Ones have not visited us in many thousand season-cycles. When one of my teams saw you a few days ago, in the cave on the cliff, we hoped. . . . But you are outworlders, surely. How did you get into the cave? From the tunnel that leads into the cliff? Did you arrive in a conveyance of your own, or did the Great Ones bring you?" There was fear in the spokesman's face now, but less fear than sorrow.

Vince's mind raced. He'd better not admit his party's

small size and helplessness. "We came in a Lenjan ship from another world, hoping to find the Lenj. We are not their enemies; we seek help from them. You say they have not visited you for a long time?"

Shontemur's small eyes peered at him worriedly. There were mutters (not hostile, Vince thought) from the other five natives. Then Shontemur smiled sadly. "You are refugees, then, from some peril. Are there many of you?"

"Enough."

Shontemur smiled more deeply. "An elastic word. Be assured, stranger, that you have nothing to fear from us— our purpose upon Wolami is simple and peaceful. We are very disappointed that you are not the Great Ones, the Lenj. There are those among us who fear the Lenj are dead, or so distantly lost they will never return. Are you pursued?"

Vince felt dazed. He glanced at Geegee, who looked intrigued, then sighed. "There's not much chance of pursuit in the immediate future. But, unless we can find the Lenj, invasion *may* come eventually. What is the—uh, I presume Wolami was once a part of the Lenjan empire?"

Shontemur made a small gesture with one hand. "Obviously. But it is the only world my people know. Whence did you come—from the near-sky, or from the great island of stars that can be seen at night in the northern latitudes?"

Slowly, gripped by a terrible disappointment, Vince said, "We came from that island of stars. Haven't you any knowledge of where the Lenj went from here—Or didn't they leave cities? Or machinery, or artifacts?"

Shontemur grinned. "I suspect you know more of their machinery than we, until we saw you in the cave, we did not know that their travel-station was in this part of Wolami. Now that knowledge will be added to the lore. Do you claim possession of it? May we come in and look?"

Vince glanced at his companions, found them grinning, and chose a noncommittal answer. "I'm not the leader of our party, but I presume there'd be no objection—since this is your world. Please believe me, we have no designs upon Wolami. We want nothing but to find the

Lenj." He paused, trying to get control of his thoughts. "Don't you have any real history of the Lenjan occupation?"

Shontemur looked shocked. "Occupation? Why, the Great Ones *built* Wolami, or refashioned it, and gave it to us, along with our Purpose. They left us what we need: speech-boxes to keep the language pure, metal for our spears and other tools, ways of making paper and scribing upon it. You speak, stranger, as if the Great Ones were conquerors! Do you then know so little about them?"

Vince sighed. "I didn't mean to imply that—we know they were very just. You speak of a purpose—what is that purpose, may I ask?"

Shontemur looked puzzled. "You do not even know that? Why, we are the Watchers!"

Vince felt hope leap within him. "Watchers? You mean you're sort of, on guard here? Then you must have some way of communicating with them—reporting, at least!"

Shontemur peered at him for a minute before answering. "We do not, stranger. If legends are true, the Great Ones formerly visited us often to examine what had been scribed. Then there was a great trouble, about which they told my ancestors little, and they came no more. But the promise was that they would someday return."

Vince turned and stared out over the desert, above which the heat-shimmer was intense now. Finally he turned back to the native. "And you've just been waiting ever since?"

"What else would we do? We wait, and scribe, and watch."

"Scribe? You keep records, you mean? Of what?"

"Why, everything!"

"Space! You have a lot of records stored up. Or do you destroy them after awhile?"

Shontemur's face closed in. "The Patriarchs decide what is to be kept, and what is to be merely abstracted. It is a crime for anyone else to destroy scribing, of course."

Vince sighed wearily. "I don't suppose . . . I wonder if

it would be permissible for us to examine some of the records—the oldest ones, I mean?"

"That," Shontemur said guardedly, but with a trace of disapproval, "is a matter I would not even undertake to consider. I am only chief of the local community, twenty twenties of Watchers and their families and a few orphans."

"Well, who *would* undertake to consider it? The Patriarchs? Where are they?"

Shontemur smiled minimally. "I could not divulge that, of course, even if I knew. Since your coming they have undoubtedly gone into hiding."

Vince fought down exasperation. "Look here—we don't intend you any harm. And we don't have any idea of interfering with your watching or your scribing. We're in a jam, and we'd like to get out of it if possible. There might be something in your oldest records—since the Lenj last visited you—that would help us. You *would* like to have us leave, wouldn't you?"

"Very much, if we were sure you wouldn't bring Evil Ones upon us."

"We aren't evil, damn it, just lost! You say your Patriarchs have moved since we got here. They must know about us, then."

"Of course. When we first saw you I sent messages to them."

"How?"

"By runner, as always. We do not possess the flying boats of the Great Ones."

"Well—can't you send our request the same way?"

"Yes, I will do that. But as I do not know where the Patriarchs will be, I cannot place a time upon the delivery."

Vince sighed. "Please do send it. Let me point this out: the sooner we leave, the less chance there is of our being pursued here. Or, at the worst, you'll be rid of *us!*"

Shontemur looked sad. "I fear that your coming will

leave our peace badly shattered in any case. Be assured, *I* will do whatever I can, within my authority, to help you leave. I *can* show you what recent scribings I retain." He half-turned and gestured north. "Were you intending to explore the canyon? If so, please let me be your guide and host, and let us pretend there is no possibility of unfriendship between us, so long as we can."

The canyon astonished Vince. It was at least two thousand feet deep; a wide, jagged cleft in solid rock narrowing to a flat bottom which, he realized, must be a soil-fill accumulated over many ages. A few weathered boulders lay strewn about, most of them half-buried. A stream, a mere thread viewed from this height, meandered along the bottom. And there was vegetation. The whole floor seemed blanketed with the pale-colored grass, while upon the banks of the stream (and covering it much of the way) were thickets. A glitter here and there attested to at least a little open water.

Back and forth across the canyon swooped broad-winged birds; apparently the same kind that hunted off the cliffs. There were smaller birds, too, and probably many more he could not see from the rim of the canyon.

The canyon floor must be about three thousand feet above the desert level, which fitted well with the height of the caves. The small stream must tumble down quite steeply to its lower course. The vanished sea, at this point, must have been unusual, with such depth running right to the precipitous edge of the continent.

He turned to Shontemur. "Do you know whether Wolami still had deep oceans when your ancestors were brought here?"

The short-legged humanoid made his small hand-gesture. "That is recorded. Wolami is as it was then. We speculate that all of us, including fish and beasts and birds, came from the same world, since there are clear relationships in skeletal structure."

Vince looked at him sharply. "Then you do have sciences? Biology, at least? How is it that . . . I mean, it seems odd that you'd continue generation after generation with no, uh, change. Hasn't the population grown? Haven't you had to strike out for yourselves into new ways?"

Shontemur smiled. "What need is there for new ways? The population is stable, regulated by the lore. We live as part of a self-perpetuating ecology. What agriculture we practice is geared to the Purpose. Land must be properly cared for to keep it fertile. Industries are adequate for our needs. Each sector is self-sufficient. When we descend into the canyon I will show you our local paper factory, and the foundry where we make our spears and other metal items. Ink is a natural product we extract from a certain bush. The cloth for our clothes"—he tugged at his own garment, showing how the ribbons separted to give ventilation—"is woven from a natural fiber. I will show you the mill."

Vince felt frustrated. "But don't things run down? You said, for instance, that the Lenj left you metal. Isn't it all used up by now?"

"There are stocks left for some time yet."

"But . . . well, what will you do when those stocks run out? Shouldn't you be learning how to smelt ores yourselves?" He watched Shontemur's troubled face. "And suppose some natural catastrophe upsets things—How would you survive? Anyway, now that the Lenj seem to be gone forever, haven't you any desire to develop as a species?"

Shontemur looked embarrassed. "It is assumed the Great Ones will return before all the metal is gone. In any case, we might make spears of wood. We only need them for hunting or for defense against the largest beasts. I do not understand what you mean by developing as a species. We have our Purpose and our life is good."

Vince sighed. "I see. Well, you say you watch and record. What do you record, if the world goes on without change?"

Shontemur looked surprised. "Why, there *is* change, of course. Animals do not pursue exactly the same life courses as their forebears. Birds do not always nest in the same places, nor fish linger in the same pools."

Vince realized he was gaping. "You mean you—you observe and record every new bird's nest that's built? Every fledgling that hatches?"

"Of course! We are the Watchers!"

"But what would the Lenj care about such things?"

Shontemur scowled uneasily. So did his five followers. "That is no proper question to ask! We record. When the Great Ones return, perhaps they will feed all the data into their computers and learn significant things. Meanwhile we have our Purpose, and our good lives, and we are happy!"

Vince, thunderstruck, stood silent. After awhile he said slowly, "We have no wish to interfere with your way of life nor violate any taboos. Forgive my questions."

Shontemur said gently, "You are a stranger, and obviously your purposes are different."

CHAPTER NINETEEN

IT WAS an hour's climb down to the floor of the canyon. A third of the way down the visitors got their first sight of Watchers at work.

A little niche had been hewed out of solid greenish rock, sufficient so that two of the natives could sit in it cross-legged, with enough of an overhang to protect them from falling rock (though not a slanting rain, if such ever occurred here). The trail led past. The two occupants gave the safari one wide-eyed scrutiny, and thereafter only glanced at it fleetingly. It seemed to be the pair's dedicated duty to keep their eyes roving ceaselessly up and down and across the canyon, except when they stared briefly at something. Each held in his lap a peculiar box-like object, apparently of leather with some slick finish on it. As Vince passed, he saw that the objects were scroll holders, with a flat writing surface across which a six-in.-wide ribbon of paper was drawn. Every half minute or so, one of the Watchers—never both at the same instant—interrupted his roving survey to ink hasty notes on the paper. When the exposed paper was full, he'd turn a small knob on the holder, rolling a new length of paper into place.

Shontemur explained that the writing implements were rods of dried-out porous wood impregnated with a semi-solid ink. Vince saw ten or so of the things sticking out of a vessel which must be the inkpot. "How fast does it dry?"

"It is dry within a few minutes. You must understand, these are only working notes. Full accounts of everything a Watcher sees, he must scribe out later when he's off active Watch. Then a third individual, usually, but not necessarily, another member of the same team, will read both accounts, and if they conflict in any way, talk to both scribers and reach a compromise."

Vince looked around. "Where are the other four members of the team?"

"We will pass them presently."

They did. A hundred yards down the trail there was a ledge where four natives dawdled, taking their ease. Two were apparently asleep. The other two might have been on guard against dangerous animals, for they had their spears handy. They stared at Vince and the ipsisumoedans, small eyes wide, but made no sound, nor did they wake their comrades.

Shontemur smiled at Vince's puzzzled look. "Shifts of active Watching are two hours. One pair must sleep, so they can stay alert when they go back on duty. Teams are relieved at dawn, midday, sunset, and midnight."

"You mean they watch at night too?"

"Of course! Life does not stop at sundown."

In mid-afternoon Vince and the three ipsisumoedans thanked Shontemur, who'd escorted them up to the canyon's rim again, and took the shortest way back to the point where they'd climbed up off the cliff. Now that Vince knew what to look for, he could see half a dozen watch-posts within sight, always in the shelter of some ledge or boulder. Shontemur had said there were other posts scattered along the face of the cliff itself.

Their own cave, it seemed, had been taboo for as long as the lore had existed.

Vince said glumly, "Well, at least we saw what the country's like. And we needn't worry about the natives, unless Shontemur and the whole lot of them are real actors!"

Geegee paused before starting down the cliff. "I doubt very much that they are capable of hostility. They don't know whether the Lenj would approve if they fought visitors like us. So long as we don't try to interfere with their Purpose! My puzzle-cog grinds, friend Vinz—Why would the Lenj establish a thing like this? Surely they are not concerned with how many birds build nests in a season!"

"Well, the Lenj have been gone a long time. Maybe at first they *did* want to watch the ecology of this world. Or maybe Shontemur's remote ancestors got the instructions garbled. Maybe, even, the whole thing started with some native chief's dream. The Lenj could have put them here merely to assure a semi-civilized planet to come back to, if they ever wished. Or maybe it was a simple act of compassion. The home world Shontemur mentions so vaguely may have suffered some catastrophe. Such as a space war."

Geegee curled his hearing-organs in affirmation. "That is possible. In any case, we may learn something if the Patriarchs decide to let us read the old records."

"Hiss-hiss-hiss!"

Gondal was vastly amused at Vince's account of the Watchers. "So the Lenj put them here to count bird's nests, eh? Well, I see no reason a few of them may not visit us. Possibly it will jog their memories."

Vince shrugged. "I'm inclined to write them off so far as being of any help. What have you and Akorra accomplished? Any progress with that Lenjan mathematics?"

Gondal turned serious. "This much: we now feel it is no simple mathematics, but rather a numerical language based upon some fundamental peculiarity of their computers. So the study turns to the computers themselves, which means cutting into the walls of the ship that brought us here. We must see the memory-banks. Oh—Akorra has made a start, no more than that, but promising, with the extraction of something in ordinary mathematics from that key-disc. We have a tentative plan to try to reeducate one of the computers to translate from our mathematics to theirs. Then, possibly, we can arrive at a program back to Shann!"

Vince eyed him impatiently. "How soon?"

"That I cannot predict. You see, it is not simply a matter of calculating to a point in our galaxy, which of course has moved considerably since the Lenj left Shann, but of translocating between two Lenjan depots. That, we are sure, is the only way. For ordinary FTL—even aside from the time needed for such a trip—the two depots may not have any useful spatial relationship to one another."

Vince shrugged listlessly. "I can believe that. I guess Geegee and I had better cultivate Shontemur after all. That doesn't seem to be any more of a dead end than *your* work."

"Hiss. I regret I cannot offer you more hope. Yes, by all means cultivate the Watchers!"

Six days passed. This was the day Shontemur had set for another meeting.

Vince, Geegee, and two warriors climbed again to the top of the cliff, taking a more lateral path, since they knew where they were going. Shontemur was already on high ground waiting, with his usual five followers. Vince raised a hand in greeting. "Hello! Is there any word from your Patriarchs?"

Shontemur made a reluctant bow. "There is, outworlder. They have pondered your situation. Two tens of runners are coming, laden with transcripts of ancient records that may bear upon your problem." The local chief hesitated. "They have done another thing, which they and I recognize as a serious gamble. They have directed me to take you to a tunnel entrance not far from here which has been taboo like the cave we first saw you in. Now the Patriarchs, who, when they are chosen, learn secrets far too precious for a mere sector chief like me, inform me that ancient secret lore describes this taboo tunnel as leading to an important place of the Great Ones. Whether there are more giant cages such as I saw when I visited you, or some other kind of machinery, is not known. I myself have stood at the mouth of the tunnel, itching with curiosity." Shontemur paused, eyeing Vince in a troubled way. "Your coming has been a great shock to them. Though you say there is little likelihood of pursuit, still it is clear that if one group of outworlders can come here, larger groups, possibly with evil intent, may come also. It has made more real to us the fear that the Great Ones have indeed vanished for all time. If that were the case, we should have no Purpose." The short-legged being sighed. "My ancestors were warned of the Evil Ones with whom the Great Ones contended, on worlds and in skies beyond imagining. Outworlder, I can comprehend the dilemma of the Patriarchs. Either they must decline to help you, risking the arrival of your enemies, or they must offer you what help is possible, risking evil intensions and acts on your part." The sector chief made a helpless little gesture. "You were honest enough, unless it be subtle deception, to admit being fugitives. We would rather place our future in your hands than in the hands of your pursuers. That is a naïve choice, perhaps, but at least we know you are not the Evil Ones against whom we were warned." He looked at Vince beseechingly.

Vince, deeply moved, stood pondering. "Well . . . where is this tunnel you mention?"

"A little way up-canyon. But first, the Patriarchs say, you must examine the transcripts. Come with me, if you will—the runners should be arriving before long; and the task of reading will not be a short one."

"Season-cycle two hundred seventy-three," the transcript read. "It is over three lifetimes since the Great Ones last visited us, taking with them all previous records and directing us to begin a new calendar. Therefore, there was much skepticism among the unfaithful when a ship of the Great Ones appeared in the sky and detached a small segment of itself which came down to us. Though no Great Ones appeared, the segment spoke in a loud voice, as follows: 'There is a great war in space, and we are terribly pressed. We must abandon certain cells of space, and Wolami is a key to several. We will return when we can. Pending that, we have tried to assure that the enemy may not find Wolami. Should he nevertheless succeed, you will know him by this description: he is taller than any of you, and bulkier. His heavy fur is of a dark-brown color. His short snout bears the teeth of a meat-eater, and though his hands are capable of grasping, they are not delicate; and his feet have claws. His eyes are small and almost hidden beneath furry brows. His ears are small and round, and set far back on the sides of his head. . . ."

Vince was staring at Geegee. "The Chullwei! The Chullwei! Do you—have you ever seen them?"

"I have indeed, friend Vinz—on the beaches of the island where I was not supposed to be. The ships you saw descending upon Weeping Woman—you said those were Chullwei. What does it mean, Vinz? Surely those beings could not challenge the Lenj!"

Vince shook his head dazedly. "I . . . don't know. From what I heard of the Chullwei, they've been known in that cell of space for as long as there's been space travel. But they weren't all that advanced! And only recently have they gotten together enough of an empire to be a threat."

"Maybe, Vinz, they had a greater past. Among my own species, tribes have grown powerful, then fallen to fighting among themselves, and diminished."

"Well, maybe so." Slowly, Vince turned back to the transcript.

"The ship's segment," the account continued, "then told us that the sun would be extinguished for a short time, but that we need have no fear. Then it went back into the sky to join itself back onto the ship.

"Some hours later the sun did go out. There was panic, even though the population around the globe had been warned. People fell upon the ground and wailed. Great bonfires were built. Many vowed that the ship was not of the Great Ones, but came from one of the evil races mentioned in old lore.

"But after less than two hours the sun came on again.

Just prior to the relighting, Wolami, in many places, shook with an awful tremor. More panic occurred, with grievous outbreaks of violence.

"There was no further message from the Great Ones, nor was the ship seen again."

Vince, finishing the transcription, stared wordlessly at it for a while. Then, his mind only half working, he picked up another from the pile and began reading it.

But there was nothing further that seemed to have any significance. "We've got to get back to Gondal and Akorra," he muttered. He looked up at Shontemur. "Can a party of us meet you here tomorrow, to go look into that tunnel?"

"As you wish, outworlder."

Gondal glided aimlessly back and forth, snakeheads pulled down near to his body, tiny eyes unseeing. After awhile he looked up at Vince. "It might simply have been a show. Hiss! If one wanted to convince a backward populace that one were a god, what better way then to turn out their sun for a while?"

Vince said impatiently, "That doesn't make any sense at all. In the first place, the Lenj never made the slightest effort to look like gods—here or elsewhere. In the second place, if you *were* trying to pose as a god, would you admit to your subjects that you were fleeing from an enemy? No, the single ship that delivered the warning—notice that it appeared in the *sky*, not in this depot—had some other reason for turning off the sun temporarily. Maybe the sun needed recharging, or something; the message flatly stated that the Lenj didn't expect to be back for a while."

Geegee put in, "Could a single ship carry enough fuel, or energy in some form, to power a sun for so many thousands of years?"

Vince looked at Akorra. She made a small gesture with one hand. "So far as we know, it's possible. Think of the energy required to bring us . . . how far? Half a million light-years? We do know that the Lenj could store fantastic amounts of energy in very small objects."

Gondal waved impatient tentacles. "You are all hopelessly romantic. But all right, for the moment let us entertain your theory. The Lenj, knowing Wolami was going to be abandoned for a long time, sent a ship to make sure this excuse for a sun was properly programmed and fueled. Why did they arrive *off* Wolami, rather than in this depot? We know the depot was in working order, for it still is!"

Geegee said, "Perhaps the Lenj did not know, however. Notice that the ship arrived two hundred and seventy-three years after the last previous visit. Perhaps it took that long getting here by some other route."

Vince said, "Two hundred seventy-three years? Those would be Wolami years—season-cycles—of course. Were the Lenj that long lived?"

Geegee chuckled. "The transcription you read did not say there were any Lenj in the ship; it said specifically that no Great Ones showed themselves. Could not the ship have been automatic, or pre-programmed, like the disc Akorra so generously brought us on Shann?"

Akorra smiled. Vince tossed up his hands. "All right, all right. Where does it all leave us?"

Gondal uncoupled from his cannister. "Hiss-hiss-hiss! It leaves us on Wolami, impatiently waiting for morning so we can go see what is in that tunnel Shontemur has promised."

CHAPTER TWENTY

SHONTEMUR led them to an ancient dry side-canyon only a few hundred yards from his village. Nothing disguised the tunnel mouth except a natural overhang of rock. There was an outpost of Watchers just across this narrow canyon, and Vince saw them staring and scribing hasty notes.

He hesitated just outside. "Will you let me go in alone for a ways, Shontemur? I want to see whether there's a faint glow that only I can see—as there is in the other tunnel."

Shontemur bowed glumly. "Do you not even want a torch?"

"No, thanks. I'll be all right." Vince stood listening for a moment, then stepped into the dark hole.

This tunnel was the same size as the other, but it didn't start off level; it slanted upward to the first turn, about twenty-five yards in, then continued to rise very gradually for a ways farther before leveling off. He advanced cautiously. It seemed to him that, despite the constant watch, some nocturnal animal might slip in and make this a lair. But he heard nothing and smelled nothing, and soon his eyes were adjusted and he could see by the faint glow.

However his eyes felt puckery, and kept twitching. He tried to tell himself that was only a result of poring over so many inked transcripts the day before.

Finally, convinced the tunnel was continuing on straight, he retraced his steps. The day light renewed the discomfort of his eyes, and he had to push aside a feeling of dull fear. He made no protest when Gondal said, "Hiss. Since

I am equipped to hold more than one flashlight easily, why do I not lead? Shontemur, you can follow behind me, then Vinz, then Akorra. You, Geegee, may have the honor of being rear guard. Hiss-hiss-hiss. Though I expect you to rally forward promptly if I encounter trouble! So. In we go!"

The little procession rounded the turns and went on along the straight tunnel. After ten minutes Geegee's big soft voice came from the rear. "My direction-cog tells me we are getting very near our own adopted chamber! Can we have overlooked some exit there?"

Vince said, "I've been thinking the same thing. Maybe there was another exit—this tunnel—at one time; but the Lenj blocked it up for some reason. Shontemur, would that fit what you know?"

Shontemur made the little hand-gesture. "Almost anything would fit what I know."

Gondal hissed impatiently, "We will never find out by languishing here. Come!"

Another five minutes, and the flashlight-beams reflected dimly off something ahead. Gondal paused for a moment. "A turn, I think—no doubt for blast-protection like the others. Now we shall—" His leg-tentacles moved faster.

They rounded the pair of right-angle turns, and the lights bored into a dark chamber. Gondal writhed free of the tunnel and swept the lights around. "Hiss! An entirely different installation! No travel cages. View-screens and dial gauges; computer keyboards like the ones we know. Nothing that—The gods! Akorra, look at those conduit-cables running into the ceiling! A yard thick! Three, four—eight of them!"

Vince stood with the others in a group just inside the chamber. It wasn't nearly as big as the one housing the translocation cages. To him, the place had the look of a communication center; but not as important a one as he'd seen on Shann. There was no special equipment such as a large sphere representing a world, or an aggregate of hexahedrons. Just dials and switches and keyboards, and those huge cables that seemed capable of carrying almost the energy output of a star. He felt letdown, hollow, a little sick. He guessed he was worrying more about his eyes than he consciously realized.

Akorra, a flashlight of her own in her hand, walked to the bank of dials. "Why, some of the needles are off the pins!"

Vince, simply because he felt sour, said, "They're probably just stuck there."

"No!" she said, "They're—Look, this one moves a little!" Gondal scuttled hugely over to join her. "Hiss. You are right! So what is it that we have—a flow of power? Shontemur—does your lore speak of yet other installations than this?"

The Watcher chief sighed. "If there is secret lore about other installations, the Patriarchs have not confided in me." He turned unhappily to Vince. "You do not seem elated. Does this place, then, promise nothing?"

Vince nodded toward Gondal and Akorra. "They are the scientists. I'm just along for the ride."

Two more days had passed.

Vince, his eyes feeling a little better, sat in the cave overlooking the desert. Also there were Akorra and two of Geegee's warriors.

He realized Akorra had said something. "I beg your pardon? I was—my mind was elsewhere."

She repeated in her quiet Nessen voice, "Gondal has explained to me about your eyes, and about his part in getting you into such a situation. He is quite bothered; he feels he has failed in a debt of honor. I told him I thought you were no longer as angry with him as you were a few days ago."

Vince resisted an urge to raise a hand and rub at his eyes. "Angry? No, I guess I'm over that. I might be just as badly off if he hadn't done it, or worse. It's been worth it, I guess." His grin felt tight and odd. "What more could I have asked, really? And it's not as if I'd been born blind. I had good eyesight for quite a few years."

She was silent for a minute. Then, "Still, you are young

—considerably younger, I think, than Gondal or I. Perhaps you are too pessimistic. Your body is healthy. Even without the medicine, you may recover and your eyes may be all right."

"Not likely, I'm afraid." He stared out over the desert. The familiar landscape, in his imagination, at least, seemed a little blurred and distorted. "But let's forget about me. Have you and Gondal come up with anything about the other installation since we last talked?"

"Nothing really significant. He seems to have lost some of his interest in it. I think this world is beginning to depress him; he's an amphibian by nature, you know, and there's so little water here. But he does have one theory."

"What's that?"

"He's almost sure the installation is somehow related to the artificial sun. During the day, when the sun passes most nearly overhead, the dial needles move the farthest, and he thinks he can hear relays opening or closing somewhere in the walls. He plans to go back with an instrument or two he's working on to see if he can learn more. He's quite ingenious, really."

He grinned without much mirth. "He is that, all right." He pondered for a minute. "We were talking the other day, remember, about that bit of local ancient history? How the Lenjan ship, possibly not manned, visited here and somehow turned off the sun for a couple of hours?"

"Yes."

He shifted his weight and stretched out one leg before him. "I've been thinking about that. Our theory was that the ship came to tend the sun, to check on its programming or something like that. I haven't been able to see how the quakes that followed tied in with that theory, unless there was some mishap involving artificial gravity or something. But now that you mention the upper installation— by the way, Geegee's paced the tunnels out, and that installation seems to be directly over ours—there does seem to be a possible tie-in between the quakes and the turning off and on of the sun. If that installation was built so that the sun could be controlled from the ground . . ."

She sat up straighter, staring at him. "Go on."

"Well. . . . Those eight big cables weren't put in just to conduct controlling currents. They'll carry something tremendous, even if it's only ordinary electricity. And remember, when we got here, the travel-depot's energy-store was depleted, and the ship had to supply its own energy to land?"

"Yes, Vinz. What are you thinking?"

"I see this as a possibility: maybe the ship *didn't* come here to regulate the sun, or to check on it. Maybe it *was* a manned ship, and maybe it needed fuel, or a supply of energy. Maybe it took what energy was stored in the artificial sun then; and maybe automatic machinery on Wolami replenished the sun from energy-stores here. That might explain the quakes somehow. If a tremendous store of energy is suddenly moved. . . . Well, I don't know. You'd be better able to judge that."

She was suddenly on her knees, halfway through the act of getting to her feet. Her voice was shaky. "Why, yes! Yes, certainly! Transfer of such a vast amount of energy would be equivalent to transferring a certain amount of mass! You can't—you couldn't—Vinz! That gives us a line on another problem that's been facing us!"

He looked at her and felt a twinge of shame that he couldn't share her enthusiasm. "Oh?"

"Yes, Vinz! We've been worrying about a source of energy . . . here. Even without the Lenjan computer-mathematics, Gondal and I have been able to calculate that there's not enough energy in the ship to take us back to Shann even if we could work out the programming. And as you mentioned just now, the installations here were drained long before we arrived. But if that upper installation could send energy *to* the artificial sun—if you're right—maybe it could bring energy back! And we could—there would be all the energy we needed!"

He watched her face twitch with excitement. The Nessen expressions weren't exactly like human ones; but there wasn't so much difference, really. He thought about the matter of the energy. A bit of excitement began to stir in him, a bit of hope.

Then he slumped, sighed. "There's an implication I don't think you'll like. *I* don't like it."

"Oh?" Her eyes moved back and forth from one to the other of his.

"Wolami," he said. "Suppose we *were* able to draw energy from Wolami's sun. What would that mean to the place? Even if we just diminished the light and warmth, only took a fraction of the energy. . . ."

Slowly, her face went lax. "Oh. The natives here. Shontemur and . . ."

He got restlessly to his feet. "And *all* of Wolami. The life-forms, intelligent or not. It's odd—not too long ago I wouldn't have cared about insects and small animals, but now I wouldn't want to kill them even to save my own life. I've . . . I guess, having lived with the sentence of death for a while, my outlook has changed. All I know is, I wouldn't want to kill a whole world." He stood still and looked down at her. "Can you calculate it out? Could we take enough energy to send us back to Shann—or to anywhere in our own cell—without depleting this artificial sun too much?"

She looked now as if she were going to cry. "I don't— we have no way of knowing how much energy's stored there. After these thousands of years, a lot of it must be used up. And to translocate a ship so far. . . . No, I couldn't begin to guess. But very likely you are right. We *would* kill Wolami!"

He grinned without humor. "Maybe that's the real meaning of the legend. If we put out the sun, Wolami— for so long as the place lasts—there would be one big night-riot."

She finished getting to her feet. For a minute she stood looking out over the desert, where the shadow of the cliff was lengthening. Then she turned toward the tunnel. "I must not be loafing here. That mathematics *can* be solved —then, perhaps, we will have alternatives."

Shontemur came again to visit the lower installation, this time with his team to scribe copious notes.

Vince watched with a feeling of compassion. What could primitive paper and ink do against the inevitable running down on Shontemur's world? He was still watching when Shontemur met his eyes and said, "I must send more data to the Patriarchs!"

Vince glanced around at the natives busily scribbling and making crude sketches. "Why," he asked, "don't the Patriarchs come here?"

The sector chief looked embarrassed. "That would not be prudent. So many things could happen here. . . ."

Vince nodded. Then, on impulse, he asked, "Tell me— you heard me quote something the other day about Wolami girding for battle. Had you ever heard it before?"

"I had not, outworlder."

"Well, what do you take it to mean? Is there anything in your lore that might explain it?"

"I think not. I have been pondering. On the hopeful side, may it not mean that if the sun should ever go out again, that the Lenj will return?"

Vince said, "Geegee expressed the same thought. It may have meant that once. But what about this: there was at least this one installation about which you yourself knew almost nothing. Might not there be others on Wolami? Couldn't one or more of them hold war machines—automatic ones that would activate themselves when the sun went out?"

Shontemur blinked at him. "Do you mean that something could rise from the ground and fight invaders? A machine could do that?"

"It's just a thought. But why not? Your sun must itself be a machine of great complexity. Could not war machines lie buried, waiting some signal?"

The sector chief looked unhappy. "I am not equipped to assess such thoughts." He stared around the chamber. "If only the Great Ones had taught us more. . . . We are loyal; we would not fail them. . . ."

"So you feel now. But civilizations, believe me, sometimes stray from reasonable courses."

"Possibly you are right," Shontemur said. He peered at Vince. "Tell me, outworlder—Why are you so deeply interested in that scrap of legend? Surely you have not found a way to turn off the sun?"

Vince felt a stab of guilty surprise. He had trouble meeting Shontemur's eyes. "No," he said, "we haven't found a way to do that. The possibility has been discussed, that's all. You understand, any further Lenjan artifacts we might find, such as war machines, might help us solve our problems and leave Wolami. Believe me, if I *could* turn off your sun and leave Wolami dark, I would not. Akorra and I have already agreed upon that point, and I think the others would too."

He hadn't realized that Geegee was standing close enough to overhear, but evidently the ipsisumoedan had been. He approached Vince a short time later. "I heard your pledge to Shontemur, friend Vinz. It occurs to me you may be pleased to know that you are right about me and my warriors, at least. They reported to me your discussion with Akorra, and we talked among ourselves. We will not murder Wolami under any circumstances."

Vince, not thinking deeply about it, remarked, "That makes it almost unanimous, doesn't it?"

"Almost," Geegee said seriously.

Vince looked at him sharply. "What do you mean? Do you think Gondal—"

"Gondal," Geegee said, "is an enigma to me. At times he seems honorable, even though he is a pirate. At other times I would not trust him with an abandoned bird's nest. And know this, Vinz, he already has the idea of pulling energy from Wolami's sun. He remarked to me that there appeared to be no other source of energy within reach sufficient to take us back to Shann, and that the upper installation might be the means of getting it. He did not sound serious, but I would not depend upon that."

Thinking it over, Vince felt a touch of his old anger

against the Onsian. "In that case, we'll simply make sure he doesn't!"

Geegee smiled. "I would join in that, friend Vinz. But Gondal is wily."

"Maybe so. But we can take the first step right now. Come on!" Vince led the way to where Shontemur was still working. "Shontemur, we have some advice for you."

The sector chief looked apprehensively from one to the other of them. "Yes, outworlder?"

"Akorra and Gondal will be wanting to study the upper installation further. Let them, within limits: but *don't* let Gondal touch a keyboard. Don't let him cut into the walls or into any of the equipment. Do you understand? Say it's taboo, say the Patriarchs have forbidden it, say anything. But make him keep his tentacles off! And keep sufficient force around to stop him if he defies you!"

Shontemur sighed. "Has this to do with our sun, outworlder?"

"Yes."

Vince, full now of painful emotions he didn't understand (unless they were simply varieties of guilt), walked away slowly. He became aware of Geegee at his elbow. "What do you think, Geegee? Did I do wrong?"

"I think not, friend Vinz. In some ways it may not have been completely right, but certainly it was not wrong."

CHAPTER TWENTY-ONE

A day later, sitting alone in the cave staring out over the desert—with eyes that definitely felt numb now, and ached vaguely much of the time—Vince was still wondering whether he was a hero or a traitor, when he heard Akorra's voice from the tunnel. "Vinz! Vinz!"

He got abruptly to his feet, forgetting himself in his concern that she might be in trouble. But before he'd gotten two steps she burst into sight, alone and apparently unharmed, squinting in the daylight. He felt suddenly angry. "You shouldn't come through the dark alone like that! You might have tripped and—"

She blinked a Nessen smile. "Oh, nonsense—I could walk that tunnel in my sleep now. We've done it, Vinz— we've broken the Lenjan math! Oh, we can't calculate in it yet, but at least the computers will answer us now!"

He stared at her, his pulse throbbing in his ears. But slowly his excitement died. "Oh. Well, that's fine. Fine. How did you do it?"

She had to gulp in a breath. "It was such a surprise! We had an experiment rigged up, with three of the ship-segment's computers isolated; we cut into the bulkheads to get at their wiring and fed them quadratic equations in ordinary mathematics, with a time-lag between computers. What we were trying to do (it was Gondal's idea) was make sure once and for all whether the things have some way of intercommunicating even without any wire connections. We needed someone for the third keyboard, and we've been able to teach Geegee enough algebra so he can handle it. Then, after we'd tried one equation with no

174

response, Geegee said, "Let me suggest something, please." And what we did was feed in an equation with the simple factors plus two sets of extraneous roots. Do you follow me?"

"More or less."

"Well, that's what we did, giving a different set of roots to each of the computers. And immediately the ship's voice—that one that seems to come from all parts of the ceiling—said very plainly, "What is desired?"

Vince tried to concentrate on her story. "Quadratics? I'd have thought you'd have tried far more complex things than that long ago!"

"We had, we had! But . . . I suspect it was Geegee's idea—the three sets of roots. It tickled something in the computers—by the way, they *can* intercommunicate without wiring connections. Now we'll—" She went silent, the life slowly leaving her expression. "You're not excited at all."

He tried to smile. "I'm very happy for you. It's just that . . . Oh, hell—it's fine. It's splendid!" He hadn't the heart to remind her that they'd still be trapped on Wolami for lack of fuel or energy. Let her enjoy her triumph.

She took him by one hand and tugged him toward the tunnel. "Please come inside. We're worried about you sitting out here all alone!"

He laughed, a trifle harshly. "Oh, I won't throw myself down the cliff. Curiosity will keep me around for a while, if nothing else. Here—let me lead; I can still see fairly well by the glow."

Gondal seemed to have conscripted Geegee as a full-time assistant. The two of them sat punching out questions on keyboards, asking the same questions verbally, and feeding whatever replies they got into different computers. The ship's segments looked like spiders' nests, with all the wires strung about.

Gondal waved a tentacle absently at Vince as he came in. Then he demanded, as if talking to the air, "How was it possible for this ship to zero into this cage, even though positions of both Wolami and Shann had changed greatly after so long a time?"

With almost no pause, the ship's voice replied, "Both askers must be heard."

Gondal writhed angrily, swiveling both snakeheads toward Geegee, who sat grinning. "Humor the accursed things!"

Geegee repeated Gondal's question. At once the mechanical voice said, "There are certain markers upon each world that serve as targets in the infra-continuum. Chronometry built into any ship's computers shows time elapsed, while motions of selected bodies within any given cell can be programmed in from the data-banks of any travel center. Such data was programmed in by Shann center. It is not a difficult calculation to predict approximate locations of destinations. Automatic machinery corrected course to Wolami in the last stages of travel."

Gondal's two heads darted looks at Akorra. "Ah! Then the key-disc did *not* contain the program from Shann to Wolami?"

"Both askers must be—"

Gondal tossed tentacles about in exasperation, but Geegee was already repeating the question. The voice replied, "What was programmed into the disc was restrictive, to prevent travel to any destination other than Wolami. Into a similar disc could have been programmed restrictions to a different destination, or to several, or an absence of restriction—that is, mere opening of the ship's hatch, and program-to-depart."

Gondal poked his heads toward Akorra. "Do you grasp that? I will wager now that we will not *have* to solve the Lenjan mathematics completely! All the programming we need to get back to Shann will be done by the computers —if only we ask the right questions in the right way! And incidentally, we seem now to have awakened these idiot computers to the point where they will accept verbal queries, without need of keyboard! He called toward the ceiling, "Is that true?"

"Both askers—"

Eventually, after some tedious questioning by Gondal and Geegee in tandem—and one brief interlude of infuriated dashing about by the Onsian—various things were established: that the Wolami travel-center's computers could reprogram the disc for return to Shann; that the ship would still perform; that there was not enough energy aboard or in the depot for the trip, and that enough enough could be drawn from Wolami's artificial sun to fill the need. Vince listened to the last item grimly. Apparently the djinn-like computers of the upper installation would deliver the energy upon a simple request properly made! He glanced at Akorra, then at Geegee.

He suddenly realized that Gondal was asking another question: "What is the significance of the legend about Wolami girding for battle?"

Geegee repeated the question.

The voice answered. "That information is not possessed."

Gondal glared, pondered, and asked, "Do you know the entire quotation?"

This time, after Geegee's repetition, there was a pause. Then, astoundingly, the voice said: "Members of your party have quoted it several times. That fact is in the data-banks. There was no record of such a legend prior to your coming."

There was a silence in the ship. Finally, in a subdued voice and after two gulps from his back-cannister, Gondal asked, "Can you hear everything said in the chamber? And . . . have you other senses for detecting what goes on?"

Geegee repeated the question solemnly, but with a suppressed grin.

The voice said, "This ship's computers automatically link with the computers of any travel-center; hence, all senses of the center are available. This particular installation possesses visual, audient, olfactory, magnetic, mass, and radio-penetrability sensors. Therefore, considerable data, and an electronic mockup, exist for each of your party. Everything you have said or done within range of the installation's sensors, or of the ship's, has been recorded."

Gondal heaved himself up, flowed like some agitated octopus from the ship, and lurched about the chamber. Finally he came to a crouch. "Hiss! Why were we so slow in finding out?"

Vince, half-amused, asked, "finding out what?"

"That we are in the belly of a monster! No—merely in its lair where it can watch us every second! He coiled his breathing-appendage, gulped air-mixture, and shouted at the ceiling of the chamber, "Get us home, do you hear? Do whatever is required to send us back to Shann! And clear out those flea-bitten Chullwei before we get there!"

There was no response. Gondal lunged toward Geegee, who was standing in the cage, just outside the ship's hatch. "Well, repeat what I said, you spear-carrying barbarian!"

Geegee chuckled. "I decline, partner and friend. There are too many implications I cannot assess—and at least one that I can assess all too clearly. No, we must find some other way than stealing Wolami's sun. I suggest we get on with our questioning of the computers. Maybe, when the Lenj last stopped here, someone dropped a remark about some hidden cache of fissionables."

Vince turned away with mixed feelings.

In the next hour, while Vince was sitting in the cave again staring out at the desert, he was joined by Gondal, who'd evidently had all his nerves could stand for a while.

"Hiss! One should not, I suppose, be surprised to find idiocy in computers. Yet, when first we elicited a response from what I now realize is a monstrous hookup, I hoped . . ."

Vince eyed the Onsian listlessly. "You don't really think the computers, working from here, could clear out the way on Shann, do you?" He drew back a little as Gondal's two snakeheads thrust toward him. "Uh . . . I suppose you know by now that all the rest of us have agreed we won't save ourselves at the expense of Wolami."

Gondal waved tentacles impatiently. "Oh, I'm not angry about that. I, too, pirate though I am, would balk at killing a whole world for selfish ends. But the nonsensical thing the computers have locked themselves into!"

Vince found himself grinning. "You mean, refusing to respond unless two individuals make the same demand in tandem? Isn't that simply a built-in safety factor or something?"

Gondal gulped another lungful of air-mixture. "I don't mean that. What is exasperating is this: it seems that, because Geegee was helping us in that ludicrously simple experiment when we first broke through, the computers locked on him, like eel-hatchlings adopting as mother surrogates the first living object they see! Now, whenever I want to consult the moronic things, I must have him beside me to repeat whatever I ask. When Akorra tries to take his place they ignore her!"

Vince thought about it briefly and laughed. "Well, what's so bad about it? Geegee will cooperate, within reason. If all that's required is the sound of his voice—"

Gondal hissed, "And his body-weight and configuration, and the gods know whatever other criteria!"

"Even so, there's no real problem, is there?"

"Perhaps not. But it is galling to depend upon a primitive to whom one had had to teach elementary algebra, to say nothing of the use of a handgun. If Akorra and I confer and decide upon some experiment to probe deeper into the computer's jealously guarded knowledge, we must take time to explain the whole idea to Geegee and persuade him to cooperate. Hiss!" Gondal paused gloomily. "The accursed things appear to be cross-guarded with more restrictions than they possess data. One, for example, prevents their giving out certain types of information unless the request itself reveals some specific knowledge of the subject. The gods! If we already knew, why would we be asking!"

Vince sighed. "What, precisely, are you looking for now?"

"Hiss. A supply of energy or fuel, for one thing. And the meaning of that legend about Wolami girding for battle. I think you may have hit upon a real thought there, Vinz Kul Lo. If we could, for instance, bring about the disinterment of war machines from the bowels of this world, would we not be justified in hoping to find them well fueled? Conceivably we might even return to Shann *armed*, ready to cope with the accursed Chullwei." He paused. "There is one bit of information we were able to draw from the computers: means exist, were the equipment available, to transfer it into the cages ready for translocation. Conversely, we can by the same means get our ship out into the open air if we wish." Gondal got another breath. "Curse this air-mixture! I did not put in enough ammonia. . . . How are your eyes feeling?"

Vince looked away from the Onsian. "They don't feel good. They ache, not badly but steadily. And when I move them fast, they get blurry and don't clear up for a while. But I'd be more than content if they'd just stay like this, and—Listen. Someone's coming through the tunnel."

Seconds later Geegee and one of his warriors emerged. Geegee stood eyeing Vince and Gondal for a minute. "I have thoughts, partners and friends, that I wish to discuss with Shontemur. We will be back before nightfall, I think."

Gondal waved tentacles sullenly. Vince watched the two ipsisumoedans climb around the edge of the cave and disappear.

Gondal heaved his bulk from the cave floor and moved around restlessly. "There, for instance, is an example. Suppose I should have another idea while he is gone? I would have to wait his return before I could consult the computers." He swiveled his heads uncertainly toward the tunnel mouth, then turned them away from it. "I do not feel like being inside anyway. Were you going to stay out here? If so, I will keep you company."

Vince nodded slowly. "I want to wait for night, to see if my dark-vision is any weaker. Not that it makes any difference, but . . ."

Gondal turned both heads toward him. "I am truly abjectly sorry, Vinz Kul Lo, that I placed you in this situation. But the stakes, as I conceived them, were high, and . . ."

Vince shrugged impatiently. "When I met you I was on my own goal line anyway. I'm not complaining."

"Hiss. A courageous attitude. Though I wish you would not give up hope so completely." Gondal's tentacles fumbled at the straps of a large canteen he'd harnessed onto himself. "I wonder if I might ask of you a favor. Would you slosh water on the anterior part of my back? There's a spot I cannot reach too well. . . ."

Vince grinned. "Sure." He got to his feet and reached for the canteen.

When he was wet-down, Gondal reached for the telephone and hissed into it sharply. Vince heard one of Geegee's warriors reply. Gondal asked, "Is everything all right in there?"

"Yes, many-limbed one. Akorra napped for a while, but now she is working on an artifact."

"Thank you." Gondal hung up, then made a shrug-like gesture to Vince.

The afternoon dragged on. They lolled there without much talk. Gondal, it seemed, had no more desire than Vince to be inside. Evening came, then dusk. Gondal stirred, acting a trifle worried. "I hope Geegee has not encountered any trouble—aside from his indispensability now, I have grown fond of the worm-eared character! I think I shall wait."

Thus it was that both of them were there when the abrupt, incredible thing happened.

CHAPTER TWENTY-TWO

WOLAMI'S artificial sun was well below the horizon. The sky was still luminous enough to shed a gray half-light on the desert and to mask the few feeble stars.

Suddenly, as if a cosmic door had slammed, there was utter darkness.

Vince came involuntarily to his feet, one hand groping for the rock wall of the cave. He heard Gondal's startled hiss, and, a moment later, the bewildered cry of some late-hunting bird along the cliff. In the shocked stillness that followed, he thought he heard other very faint cries—tiny terrified protests from a myriad of small creatures. But that might have been his imagination.

Gradually, his eyes adjusted. When he could see the stars they looked blurry, but that was no surprise. He blinked his watering eyes and finally achieved some clarity; he saw the desert by familiar starlight.

But a ways out on the desert there was something unfamiliar.

He gasped and strained his eyes, trying to get them in better focus. The thing, like a hump-topped mesa, must be about ten miles from the cliffs and a half mile in diameter. Then he saw that it was still growing—not upward (the slightly humped-up top remained, more or less steadily) but to the sides! Those sides roiled and hesitated and rushed on, as if—

He realized that the voice whispering in fear and disbelief was his own. He clawed his way around the lip of the cave, ready to scuttle up the cliff like some fear-maddened insect.

Then he got control of himself and turned back into the cave. "Gondal! The telephone! Where's the—" He groped his way in the right direction, stumbled over one of the Onsians leg-tentacles, drawing a panicky hiss, found the telephone and shouted into it, "Akorra! Anybody! All of you get out of there as fast as you can run. There's a—something has—the desert's being flooded! The ocean's coming back! A spout that you could never—"

Then, as suddenly as it had vanished, the dusk was back again. He felt one of Gondal's tentacles whip around his shoulders. "What in space, Vinz Kul Lo! Can you see—the gods! Look at it!" The tentacle pulled away. "I must go inside and—"

Vince swallowed and got his voice working again. "Relax! Even a spout like that can't fill the whole planet instantly. We're well up on the cliff here. But get them out of the installation; there's no telling how far up it'll come!"

Dazed, through a red pounding film of blood, it seemed, he watched the monstrous upwelling. He heard Gondal hissing into the telephone and the faint response that promised that Akorra and the ipsisumoedans would hurry.

And now, just reaching the cliffs, came the sound of the thing, like a thousand cataracts, a thousand jet bombers. He realized he was bathed in sweat and wiped the back of his hand across his eyes. In silent awe, he stood beside Gondal, staring. The boiling front was coming with incredible speed. As the area of inundation grew, of course, the depth was much less—but still sufficient to wipe from sight the line of trees along the waterway, like ink, or rather like gray dishwater, flooding over a chalk mark.

The boiling-up in the center was not lessening.

Gondal, in his distraction, got one of his snakeheads on either side of Vince. "Look! What is that, tumbled along by the wave front? Is it—the gods; it is! A ship of some kind, swept along like a toy! And—and—more of them! Space, Kul Lo—we toyed with dreams of Lenjan war-apparatus, tearing itself from the bowels of Wolami. But these are spaceships—whole flotillas of them, and all derelicts, all ancient! Vinz! The legend—Wolami's lamp was indeed extinguished for a few minutes, and *this* is the result! How—who—"

Vince grunted a curse. "Isn't it clear enough? Geegee did it. That's what he wanted to talk to Shontemur about —if he bothered to talk to him at all. *He* turned off the sun. *He* did it!"

Gondal's heads withdrew sharply. "Hiss! That is— Hiss! Vinz Kul Lo! The computers in the upper installation. Geegee must have hit upon the required procedure to activate them. Hiss! The ingrate! The treacherous, scheming savage!"

Vince laughed raggedly. "Oh, come, Gondal! Hasn't he done precisely what we wanted? Hasn't he split the problem right through the middle? Somewhere in the west— barring some mishap that I'd bet a thousand to one against —Wolami's lamp is shinning again as brightly as ever. Geegee wouldn't have gambled; he somehow made sure first. If he got the computers to talk to him . . ."

For a minute he could hear Gondal gulping air-mixture. Then the Onsian's breathing-appendage came loose from the cannister with a hasty sucking sound. "Hiss-hiss-hiss! Oh, hiss-hiss-hiss! You are right, Vinz Kul Lo. What simpletons we are! What eel-heads! Of course! The legend did *not* say that the lamp must *remain* extinguished! Oh, hiss-hiss-hiss!" Gradually, Gondal sobered. "But what now, biped? Will the Lenj shortly descend upon us—or follow those space-wrecks out of whatever devil's hole that water is coming from? Or will someone else than the Lenj— *something* else—arrive to see who dares tamper with the lamp of Wolami?"

Vince hardly heard him. He was staring toward the rapidly nearing wave front. Its sound, blended with the more distant thunder of the central upwelling, made it necessary for him to shout. "Gondal! Gondal! Some of those derelicts are *Chullwei* ships! Or—no, I can see differences. But the basic design is the same!"

"Hiss! Is that to be wondered at, Vinz Kul Lo? The ancestors of the Chullwei—those fleabags on Shann must be degenerate descendants—were the ancient enemy. What we are seeing, two-legged one, is the debris of some cosmic battle. How it came to be lying on the bottom of Wolami's pilfered oceans—For is this not Wolami's ancient sea returning?—is a speculation to drive one insane!"

By the time surf lapped a thousand feet up the cliff from the former desert level, the overall depth of the reborn sea was enough to muffle that cosmic thunder from the ingress. Water was still coming in—there was a hump, hundreds of feet high, marking the spot—but back-pressure must be slowing it a little now. Wolami's sun, as bright and hot as ever, poured down as if beginning the senseless task of trying to dry up this uninvited wetness. Already, clouds were visible in the east.

The whole party, except Geegee and his one warrior, was crowded into the cave. Gondal poked unsteady snake-heads toward Akorra. "Do we have, madame, instruments from which we can fashion a gadget for measuring radio-activity? I am anxious to be about examining some of those wrecks. But I do not wish, at this stage of our adventure, to immerse myself in deadly water!"

Vince waited until Akorra murmured a dazed affirmative. Then he said, "Aren't you being a little optimistic, Gondal? Even if there *is fuel*—fissionables, or something else—in those derelicts, we aren't likely to get at it. The most shallow water over any of them, I'd say, is something like two thousand feet. And we don't have any submarines."

"Hiss-hiss-hiss. You forget, friend Vinz, that I am not a water-shunning dry-land creature like the rest of you. Geegee may have outthought all of us, and put himself in a hero's spot—let us hope, not a martyr's. But *I* can get at those wrecks! I cannot dive instantly to two thousand feet depth, of course, but by descending slowly I can do it. I can, perhaps, even plumb the deepest spot, where the spout comes up—if it is not deeper than three thousand feet!"

Vince was feeling letdown now. His eyes held a small,

but maddeningly constant, ache. "So—what if we get fuel of some kind? The Chullwei are probably swarming like ants inside that mountain on Shann. What would we do—just barge in and tell them they all have to leave, because the good guys are back now?"

"Hiss. I have been toying with deceptions we might plan. And the notion that intrigues me most does, indeed, involve making them think the good guys, as you put it, are back! Some of those dumbbell-shaped ships, Vinz, that you yourself said were unmistakably like the Chullwei design, may be repairable. Is it not probable that—beholding suddenly the arrival of ships nearly, but not quite, familiar—those walking flea-havens on Shann might, for a moment at least, be frozen with surprise?"

CHAPTER TWENTY-THREE

IT SEEMED later to Vince that he spent the next several days in a sort of trance, with events piling themselves one upon another faster than he could assimilate them.

The first bewilderment was that Geegee was now able to invoke the services of the installation's computers all by himself, without the need for any tandem partner. Gondal, scowlingly, speculated that this was a result of Geegee's having seen the only individual to work both with the computers of the lower installation and of the upper. Akorra, who seemed to trust the ipsisumoedan completely, was more amused than annoyed. Geegee, on his part, was more than tactful. If anything he was more humble and cooperative than ever. He seemed almost abashed by the results of what he'd done.

Shontemur visited the lower installation again, and Vince learned that no Watchers—none of the local or nearby communities, at least—had been caught by the sudden upwelling of water. With the temporary turning-off of the sun decided upon (after thorough consultation of the computers), Shontemur had signaled his teams to start home, even though no relief teams replaced them.

Then there was the breakthrough when Akorra, Gondal, and Geegee got the computers to translocate the Lenjan ship out into the open, to become the necessary work-vehicle for hauling in whatever Gondal found submerged about the still-open "portal." That strange doorway, they learned, did not open onto the core of Wolami. Only a few dozen feet below the former desert level, there was some incomprehensible plane of transference that must connect with some far-distant world. At night, as the ship hovered over the area, Vince could see the familiar purplish-blue glow.

He wondered whether that other world so strangely coupled to Wolami were an inhabited one. No fish or other animal life had come through with the water, no fossils of any kind. Only the blasted relics of a great ancient battle, it seemed, had been swept through— some still bearing the grisly remains of their crews. How, he wondered? By draining through a hole in some suddenly punctured sea bottom?

However they'd come, there were quite a number—and not all were badly damaged!

After a few days of work, Gondal sent up more than a dozen small hulls, all air tight so that he had to do nothing but take down tanks of air under great pressure and bleed them into the hulls. That idea replaced the first one of getting the Watchers to chop large numbers of treetrunks for pontoons.

The Onsian showed no ill effects of his deep immersion. He would take an hour to descend, stay down for a dozen hours while Geegee's warriors sent things down on cables, then ascend somewhat more rapidly. Apparently his species suffered nothing like the "bends" that would have crippled or killed a man.

Vince, whose eyes were steadily weakening (though the ache was mostly replaced now by numbness), was still in his apathetic daze when a small ship, dumbbell-shaped like the Chullwei ships he'd seen on Shann, bobbed to the surface—and, before his blurry eyes, kept rising! He and the others watched open-mouthed while it lifted to a thousand feet, circled, and descended again to the water, where it floated. Vince became aware of Geegee beside him. The ipsisumoedan wordlessly thrust a rupter-rifle, or some Lenjan weapon like it, into Vince's hands. Vince, his midriff heavy with apprehension, gripped the weapon and peered at the alien ship. Were there—could there be—living creatures in it? Or were ancient computers controlling it?

A hatch, obviously power-operated, opened slowly. Gondal, octopus-like, climbed out.

"Hiss-hiss-hiss!" The Onsian's chuckle came over the radio. "How is this, my friends. Do I not fly deftly with a completely alien set of controls?"

Vince went limp with relief and heard Geegee's deep chuckle beside him.

There was the feverish period while the Lenjan installation's computers were badgered into translocating some of the alien relics into the great chamber. One—the dumbbell-shaped spaceship—went into a cage, materializing as if by magic in the shallow cradle that had waited so many eons to be used again. Akorra, surrounded now by more artifacts than she could inventory, let alone study, seemed as dazed as Vince.

Gondal, his diving finished, was all over the chamber, gulping hasty breaths, climbing over reclaimed wreckage and poking his snakeheads into not-yet-dry holes, babbling ideas, and tugging and hauling at various pieces of equipment. Finally he began work on the dumbbell-shaped vessel in the translocation cage. The white-hot glare of welding and cutting (an activity seized upon by the ipsisumoedans, under Gondal's impatient tutelage, like a new delightful game) kept the chamber aflicker with uneven light. Vince, when he wasn't needed to help, stayed outside because the shifting light bothered his eyes.

Akorra, less busy than Gondal, kept Vince up-to-date on the progress. "The Lenjan ship that brought us here is capable of consuming the fissionables we've gathered from derelicts, and transforming it into the form of stored energy the Lenj used. But, for the physical handling and feeding in of the fuels, complex regulatory equipment must be devised. Also, the dumbbell-shaped vessel, if it is to take us to Shann, must undergo much alteration. Gondal is, I will swear, a mechanical genius! Though I wish he were more patient with Geegee and the poor warriors."

Vince, determined not to be a pall upon the spirits of his companions, tried to be interested. "But how can that ship—without Lenjan computers—zero in on Shann? And can it possibly have enough energy stored into it?"

She said, "That is one of the biggest difficulties. To build energy-storage units of the Lenjan type would require the transmutation of something into an artificial metal, and that is a job far beyond the capacity of the equipment we have. What Gondal is doing is installing fuel-storage tanks in the dumbbell-shaped vessel, and transferring to it the equipment from the Lenjan ship that can transform the fuel to energy of a usable kind. Also, of course, we must cut one of the computers out of the Lenjan ship and install it." She blinked her smile. "I wonder whether, when everything is installed, there will be any room for passengers."

Vince sighed. It was hard for him not to show how ridiculous he felt the whole project was. "Does Gondal— do you; you're the physicist—really think a completely alien drive system can be controlled by the Lenjan equipment? Pinpointing one translocation center from another must be something like hitting an insect in flight, with a rifle bullet at extreme range."

"Far harder than that, really," she smiled. "But the drive is not so alien; it is very much like the Lenjan one. I would call it a slightly inferior copy. I suspect that the ancient enemy (an isolated detachment of whom must have been the ancestors of the Chullwei) were a less advanced race, in contact with the Lenj, who stole ideas from them and prepared in secret for a war. Some known scraps of Lenjan history tell of such a treachery."

Vince rubbed absently at his eyes. "I see." He stared out over the reborn ocean, which, today, was gray and choppy. Wolami's climate apparently hadn't sorted itself out yet. "Gondal told me he was insisting that you stay here, with a few of the ipsisumoedans. Have you and he decided about that yet?"

She was slow in answering. "Yes. I have agreed, though I don't feel happy about it. What do you think, Vinz?"

"I think you'd better stay here. If you came with us, and things went wrong, we'd all be dead. Or at least, captives of the Chullwei. If you stay here, you can continue to study the Lenjan equipment. The ipsisumoedans will make good mechanics, with a little instruction, and Shontemur's people will help."

She blinked twice, slowly, in affirmation. "Gondal used the same arguments. But I think I shall go mad, left here."

"We'll come back for you, of course. Or somebody will."

She smiled. "If you aren't all killed, or lost forever."

"Even so."

She sighed. "Yes, the logic cannot be denied." She looked at Vince sadly. "Are you sure your eyes are not going to get well by themselves? You could stay here too. I—this may sound bigoted, but I would find you more congenial than the ipsisumoedans, though they are admirable. Your species and mine are much more alike."

He shook his head slowly. "My eyes aren't going to get well. And I'm an essential part of Gondal's plan, if my dark-vision's still adequate when we get to Shann. Also, I —well, I guess I just want to be in on the fight, if there is one."

She sighed. "A male of my own species would feel the same, I think. Well, I shall stay here and work. Even though the computers may not respond to me, without Geegee present, I have already learned a lot of theory from them. Another thing—though Gondal has not mentioned it, I am sure it is in his mind—someone must stay here and hold the fort. It is possible, is it not, that the Chullwei on Shann may also solve the technology, and that they'll be arriving here? They are not bad scientists; those of them not involved with the military dictatorship. And maybe I could—well, do something."

He peered at her, his eyes suddenly more watery than usual. Such a delicate creature to speak of holding a fort!

He said unsteadily, "I promise you we'll try very hard to get back here, or send someone."

But of course he had very little hope that they'd succeed. It didn't matter to him very much personally—he was pretty much resigned by now. But he felt very badly about Akorra.

CHAPTER TWENTY-FOUR

"Translocation to Shann has begun."

The mechanical voice seemed to have withstood its transplantation without change. Vince, gripped in a sense of unreality, sat listening to it. Were they actually under way? Could this crudely rerigged, hastily patched-up ancient ship, with nondescript tanks and pipes and motors and pumps welded onto all suitable interior surfaces like the work of some drunken wasp, *really* be hurtling through the infra-continuum, already scores of light-years from Wolami? Or was it all some dream, and delirium?

Feeling a need to reassure himself it *was* real, he turned to Gondal. "The Nesse only taught me a few words of Chullwei. You say you know a lot more. But your voice isn't right. Who's going to do the talking, if we *do* materialize inside the mountain?"

"Hiss." Gondal poked one head in the direction of Geegee. "Our computer-wooing comrade there. His voice has nearly enough the right timber. And if he has to spend this whole trip learning Chullwei, maybe it will keep him out of mischief."

Geegee chuckled. "I do not expect to be fluent in the language. If, as you say, they have no history of their ancestors, it will be convincing enough for them to hear a few garbled words. More convincing than if someone spoke to them in perfect Chullwei." He glanced at Vinz. "How are your eyes holding up?"

Vince shrugged. "All I can do is rest a lot on this trip, and hope. But there's one thing we haven't discussed. Suppose there *is*—as we've somehow decided to expect—

no light in the chamber when we materialize, except the glow that I'll presumably still be able to see by. We'll have view-screens on—but how will I be able to see anything on them? They won't pick up anything, you know. And if I step outside the ship, the whole deception is finished. I don't look like a Chullwei!"

"Hiss-hiss-hiss." Gondal heaved himself up and glided to a floor-level cabinet wedged between fuel-storage tanks. "I gave that some thought before we left Wolami." He opened the cabinet, reached in with two tentacles, and hauled out what looked like an oversized diving-suit. "Remember this, that I found in one of the derelicts? It would fit a Chullwei comfortably enough. You, Vinz, may rattle around in it a trifle, but you should be able to walk. And, with your face smudged dark so they cannot see you inside—"

"Hold on!" Vince got to his feet, scowling at the Onsian. "What are you talking about? Do you mean you want me to climb out of the ship, assuming we ever get there at all, wearing that monstrosity? I thought Geegee was going to do all the talking!"

"Ah, hiss. He shall, by radio. But *you*, Vinz, will be able to see, if the chamber is dark. You will have a private radio frequency for reporting to us. . . ."

"Huh. You have everything figured out, don't you? What if the chamber's not dark? What if it's lit, and swarming with Chullwei scientists—or soldiers?" Vince met Geegee's amused eyes. "Oh, all right, I guess it's logical. I *am* the most expendable. I'm pretty far gone anyway."

"Hiss. One thing is certain—you are the most pessimistic! We do not know what we will find inside the mountain. We must simply prepare as cunningly as we can, and act according to the scents in the current. Have we not fangs?" Gondal gestured toward certain jury-rigged controls of Lenjan weapons they'd installed in the ancient hull. "If we use to the utmost whatever few moments we are granted . . ."

Vinz shrugged listlessly. "All right—I'll climb out and

reconnoiter, and be the first target if it comes to that. *You* supply the wits!"

The trip was, in hours, about the same length as the earlier one. To Vince it felt a thousand times longer.

He roamed the ship, almost desperate with tension. He ate too much because of the gnawing in his middle, got bloated, and had to limit himself. He held grimly to a schedule of sleep—though "sleep," more often than not, consisted of tossing, wide awake. Vaguely, he worried about his total lack of hope. And, after the first few hours, he kept going on simple stubbornness. He made some effort to avoid being surly with his companions, but didn't succeed very well; and he didn't even bother to try to act cheerful.

Somehow, though, he survived. And he did feel a stir of excitement when, after what seemed a universe of time, the calm mechanical voice said, "Translation is complete. We are zeroing in on Shann travel-center."

The ship's lights were out so that Vince's eyes could adjust to darkness.

The ludicrously oversize suit, for all the spare room in it, felt unbearably stuffy. He was perspiring, and the suit did nothing about that except to exhaust a trickle of air and replace it from compression-cannisters. He waited near the only airlock Gondal had gotten into working order, feeling the sickness of simple fear. Fear? What had he to lose? Nevertheless he *was* afraid, wishing very fervently that he were somewhere else—back on Earth, back on Wolami, anywhere. He felt so weak he wondered if he could move the suit when the moment came.

The mechanical voice said, "Materialization complete."

Vince's hands clenched in the suit's gauntlets until his fingers ached. He heard Geegee's deep voice uttering harsh Chullwei phrases. A pause, then a repetition of the message. It was purposely vague—a statement of a commanding officer's name, a numerical designation of the ship, a request for a reply if the message were heard.

195

Geegee ran through the phrases a third time, then stopped. Vince heard Gondal's alerting hiss, then the inner door of the lock began to slide open. The sound was a rumble, not a rasp—Gondal had done a good job of lubrication—but the deck trembled with the mechanical force. Vince felt an abrupt minor change in weight as the ship's artificial gravity system went off, leaving him under Shann's natural tug. He made a mighty effort and got himself moving; stepped into the lock and waited out the eternity while the inner door ground shut behind him. The outer one began to open. . . .

His eyes felt puckery, and watered badly, as he darted glances about the familiar chamber. Things were blurred, but he could see that some of the apparatus was gone— clean cuts showing where supports and cables had been lasered through. Spots on the now-half-empty wall glowed more brightly than the rest of the chamber—meaning, perhaps, that there'd been some spill of extra energy when things were cut away. He wondered vaguely whether there'd been any catastrophes. No serious ones, obviously.

But of the Chullwei (or whoever had dismantled things and hauled them away) there was no sign. Had they prudently fled Shann with their spoils? Or did they lurk in hiding, weapons trained on the newly arrived ship?

The outer door was fully open now. Jaw set, he stepped forward, reached for outside handholds (feeling, through the gauntlets, the still-lingering cold of space), and lowered himself the few feet to the floor. He stood peering about, remembering to act bewildered.

There was no movement in the chamber.

He spoke very quietly through his suit radio. "There's no light except the energy-glow. Things have been taken away. I think—Yes, the whole translocator cage on the end of the line away from us is gone! They must have cut that into a thousand pieces to get it out of here!"

Geegee's voice said quietly, "Or learned how to translocate big pieces out."

"I suppose so. There are sections cut out of the walls,

and of the floor. The doors in the elevator column are closed. The whole place looks deserted."

That calm statement reflected none of the things Vince's jangling imagination conjured up. Behind the elevator column, for instance. Or in any of the tunnels. "I'm going to walk around a little. Shall I use a light?"

Gondal's voice said, "Hiss! Of course! You must act as if you were blind in the dark. But do not let any light shine into your faceplate!"

"All right." Vince fumbled for the flashlight hooked onto the suit and pressed the switch. The sudden beam of light made his eyes twitch again. Slowly, he turned about, swinging the light, pausing now and then as if studying installations. "Still no reaction. What now?"

Geegee chuckled. Gondal hissed uncertainly. "That is a question. The last thing I expected was that the Chullwei would be gone! It is not unreasonable, though—here, they would be very vulnerable. Well—if they *are* here, playing the game cunningly, they can wait longer than we. Therefore—if you find nothing blocking the tunnel to the surface, I think we must leave the ship. If we can reach Geegee's tribe they will help us get to the island—"

"Where," Vince said petulantly, "Either the Vred or the Chullwei will be waiting for us."

"Hiss! Is there any way to avoid that risk? The medicine you need, Vinz Kul Lo, is hidden underwater near the island. I consider that an objective of the first importance!"

Vince felt a stab of exasperation. He'd been so close to the medicine, then! "All right, I'll go into the tunnel far enough to see around the turns, and come back. Can I take this damned suit off now?"

"Not yet, Vinz. But when the rest of us leave the ship, then there will be no further point in your disguise."

Vince, thrusting his fear from him as well as he could, walked toward the tunnel. There'd be the smaller chamber a little way along, then the climb to the exit. What would they do about the stones piled atop it? He felt a desire to laugh hysterically at the irony of that problem. After coming so far! But he supposed they'd solve the problem some-how.

He rounded the turns, and paused where he could peer into the lesser chamber. Here, too, things had been re-moved—the mockup that represented the ancient empire, for one thing. He stared hard at the opposite tunnel, saw nothing, and stood for a minute wondering if he should go any farther. He decided not—his companions must be gnawing their fingers in anxiety.

Ten minutes later he gratefully let Geegee help him out of the suit. "Whew—I'm glad that's over! Shall we go now?"

Gondal waved an agitated tentacle. "As soon as you are able to see in the dark again! Or if you wish me to lead, I can grope—"

"No. Let's go!" Vince put out his flashlight and started blindly toward the tunnel. He felt for it, entered, and heard Gondal slithering nearby. "Here—give me a ten-tacle. All right? Are we all here?" He felt the Onsian press a beamer-pistol into his hand.

Vince's pulse was hammering now. That medicine—out there in the channel. So close now! He led off, tug-ging at Gondal's tentacle. Hope was a raging fire in him now. He'd lived so long without it. . . .

They went through the smaller chamber, made the turns in the far tunnel, and reached the beginning of the up-slope. He could hear his companions breathing heavily behind him, as excited as he was. It certainly looked as if—

Abruptly, the tunnel was flooded with light.

Vince involuntarily threw up a hand before his eyes. He heard Gondal hiss, "Down! As flat as possible! Crawl back, but keep weapons ready. If we can reach the ship—"

But the whole mountain, it seemed, was alive with sound now—shouts, the creaking of some wheeled thing, the pounding of heavily shod feet. He peered ahead and saw what looked like a steel barrier completely blocking the tunnel, solid except for small holes through which gun barrels projected. He began to squirm backward.

But it was from behind them that the amplified voice blared—Zarpi's voice. "Stay where you are for the moment! We would prefer to take you alive if possible. You have information I want. If you give it, I shall have no reason to harm you—but I will kill you if you resist."

Gondal whispered sibilantly, "He thinks we may not know about the Chullwei! Pretend we are decieved . . ."

Zarpi's voice resumed. "Vinz Kul Lo? I have reasoned out that you are not what you pretended, and that you had something to do with whisking Akorra away. And you, Gondal—you I would suspect even had I no direct evidence! But I do not hold senseless grudges. Leave your weapons and come back to the smaller chamber."

Vince, insides churning, got slowly to his feet. "What's happened?" he asked Gondal in a tense whisper. "Maybe the Chullwei never got this place after all!"

Gondal hissed sharply. "Do not be deceived! The Chullwei are noted for torturing information out of prisoners, then executing them at once. He must have reached an agreement with them, to try to persuade us to surrender!"

Vince, weary enough to drop by now, eyed the Onsian and the ipsisumoedans listlessly. "I don't know how the rest of you feel—but I've reached the end of my rope. I'm going to walk in there, but I'm not going to surrender."

Gondal's snakeheads were weaving in fury. "I agree, my unfortunate partner. Let us throw down the heaviest of our weapons, but conceal the smallest. Geegee, I can demand nothing of you nor your warriors."

The ipsisumoedan's big face was calm. "Warriors do not surrender, nor does the son of a chief. Let us go in, and conscript what company we can for the Long Journey."

And now a roar filled the tunnel, a bellow of anger from the throat of some large, impatient being. "That is enough! Zarpi, you idiot—you have failed, as I predicted. You vermin in there—do you think, perhaps, that I am too stupid to have installed listening and seeing devices? Throw down those puny handguns you carry, all of you, and march—or you will roast slowly where you are!"

Zarpi made one more try. His voice, shaky now with anger and frustration, said, "They *can* be taken alive! In five minutes I can have gas pumps here—"

"Silence, cretin!"

Vince, gripping his handgun as if it were the last thing he'd ever touch—which it almost certainly would be—forced his tired legs to carry him toward the lesser chamber. There was one more bellow from the Chullwei, who must be in a position of command, but Vince ignored it. He reached the chamber, saw the mouth of the tunnel opposite blocked with a barricade like the one in the other direction, and paused for an instant, hot rage sweeping over him because there was nothing he could shoot at sensibly. He heard Geegee's grunt of frustration and Gondal's angry hiss. He took one step into the chamber, raising his weapon; he sent its beam slashing across the barricade with no result except a shower of sparks and a glowing line across the metal. He saw one of the gun barrels—remotely controlled, no doubt—move an inch to bear on him. He went rigid, waiting for someting to slam into him. . . .

And then, though he felt no impact, something very odd happened to him. There was a quick dizziness, and his muscles seemed to have turned into wood. He realized he was falling and could not thrust out his hands to break the fall. He could, he found, turn his head and jerk it back so that it didn't strike the floor too hard. He heard other thuds behind him—the ipsisumoedans falling too, he supposed—and one last half-strangled hiss from Gondal. . . .

And then there was a period of sleep that was not quite sleep. At times he struggled to make his muscles move; he could not. Nor could he speak. His breathing was a slow, regular thing, not under his control. He could see, more or less, at times.

He was aware of great gray forms moving about the chamber. They were, he realized drowsily, ipsisumoedans.

But they were somehow wrong. Their fur was clipped, or shaved. They wore civilized clothing, carried things that looked like highly advanced implements or weapons, spoke Lenjan, and moved about, in ways subtly different than Geegee did.

He was awake enough to know that they picked him up and placed him on a stretcher and took him somewhere. And somehow one of them got his attention long enough to explain that he was only in a state of body-stasis that would wear off before long.

He saw Gondal carried by, laughably unfamiliar with his limbs all piled limply atop him and his snakeheads, eyes closed, on top of his limbs. Geegee was there, too, on a stretcher, and his warriors.

And, before he was too deeply asleep to think consciously, he reasoned it out: these strange ipsisumoedans were *Lenj*. Somehow, the brief turning-off of Wolami's sun—or perhaps the disappearance of a sea from some other world somewhere—had summoned them.

And that odd fact, on Wolami, of the computers responding to Geegee—Gondal must have been wrong in his explanation of that. Was it not, surely, that the computers found Geegee's size and shape, and the gods knew how many other things, *proper?*

Vince slept. . . .

CHAPTER TWENTY-FIVE

Port-of-Shann was well lighted. What damage the Chull-wei invasion had done was already repaired. Most of the colony's erstwhile guests were long gone. So, of course, were the Vred and the Chullwei.

Geegee and Vince stood at one side of the field, watching Akorra board a Nessen ship to go home. Geegee placed a big hand on Vince's shoulder. "My intuition-cog tells me, my friend, that you, as I have, are mulling over certain thoughts about that charming female."

Vince grinned a red-faced grin. "Well, yes. But I don't think anything's ever going to come of them."

Geegee chuckled. "Nor I. As the son of a chief, it would not be proper for me to undertake such experiments. Where, Vinz, will you go now?"

"Home, I guess. For a while, at least. And you?"

"I will be busy here for a time, teaching my tribesmen some of the things I have learned. The Lenj are going to leave Shann in our hands, except for this field and the travel-center inside Weeping Woman—which may or may not continue to be their only portal into this cell of space. They will not, in any case, reoccupy the cell as masters. Did you know that the cell was lost to them completely— that I and my warriors were to them, when they first glimpsed us, an ancient legend come to life? So were those Chullwei, whose remote ancestors the Lenj eventually overcame elsewhere. Wolami, too, was only a legend."

Vince mused for a while. "That must have been a great drama your own ancestors lived through—with a ship waiting for them, and they unable to reach it. Do you know the details?"

"No, Vinz Kul Lo. But obviously they survived. By the way, have you talked to Gondal within the last hundred hours?"

"No—before he left, he was too busy conferring with the Nesse, making sure they paid him enough for various services so he'd show a profit on this whole thing."

"Ah. Then I saw him more recently than you—and I have a message for you. He told me to say that, though things may change somewhat, there will for a long time be remote regions of this cell where persons of daring and talent may find fortune. Not to mention the possibility that the Lenj may allow a certain amount of travel to other cells. He reminds you that your dark-vision will continue to be a thing of great uniqueness, potentially very profitable. He says that when you are ready to come into space again, you can reach him through the Nesse if you are so inclined." Geegee grinned. "If you do, perhaps you will drop by here, and I will see whether I am able to go along." He paused. "You are going home to report. Will you tell them everything?"

Vince watched Akorra's ship rise on gravs and dwindle toward the stars. "There she goes. . . . You mean, about my dark-vision? I suppose I ought to. But I didn't tell the Nesse, and Akorra promised she wouldn't either. What do you think, Geegee? Do I have a right to keep a thing like that to myself? Can I honorably be that selfish?"

The ipsisumoedan chuckled. "That is a delicate question, Vince. But honor, is it not a personal thing? In cases, I mean, where the welfare of others is not directly affected. And have you not earned your dark-vision?"

Vinz grinned. "I guess so. At least, there were times when I thought I was going to pay highly for it."

Geegee curled ear-tentacles in agreement. Then he grinned down at Vince. "I must leave now, friend from the stars. My father will be impatient. I hope this is not our last meeting, Vinz Kul Lo." He thrust forward a big hand in the human gesture Vince had taught him.

Vince, a tightness in his throat, grasped the hand.

A minute later he stood watching the big gray-pelted humanoid walk away. Then he himself turned to stroll aimlessly along the border of the field. He'd be taking his own ship back to Earth as soon as supplies were loaded. That ship, primitive though it might be in space, nevertheless had the FTL drive that would be the payment of the Nessen debt to him and to Earth.

He hoped Earth's scientists wouldn't spend too long studying it, before they built their own versions of it. For sometime, not too far in the future, he intended to climb into that ship and leave the solar system again, without official company.

How many of these great science fiction stories have you read?

DEATHWORLD 3 60c
by Harry Harrison

ASIMOV'S MYSTERIES 60c
by Isaac Asimov

THE COSMIC RAPE 60c
by Theodore Sturgeon

THE KILLER THING 50c
by Kate Wilhelm

PATH INTO THE UNKNOWN 60c
by Judith Merril

THE PEOPLE TRAP 60c
by Robert Sheckley

10th ANNUAL EDITION OF
THE YEAR'S BEST SCIENCE FICTION 75c
by Judith Merril

11th ANNUAL EDITION OF
THE YEAR'S BEST SCIENCE FICTION 75c
Edited by Judith Merril

THE JUDGMENT OF EVE 50c
by Edgar Pangborn

TIME PROBE 75c
by Arthur C. Clarke

ALL ABOUT VENUS 60c
Edited by Brian Aldiss

DIMENSIONS OF MIRACLES 50c
by Robert Sheckley

EARTHMEN AND STRANGERS 50c
Edited by Robert Silverberg

FUTURE TENSE 60c
by Richard A. Curtis

THE STATUS CIVILIZATION 60c
by Robert Sheckley

THE TIME TWISTER 50c
by Emil Petaja

If you cannot obtain copies of these titles at your local bookseller, just send the price (plus 10c for handling and postage) to Dell Books, Box 2291, Grand Central Post Office, New York, N.Y. 10017. No postage or handling charge is required on any order of five or more books.

Science fiction at its best . . .

11th
Annual
Edition

THE
YEAR'S
BEST
SF

An anthology of thirty-seven stories
ranging from humorous fantasies to
tales of terror and the supernatural.
For more than a decade, Judith Merril
has selected the year's greatest science fiction and fantasy for her fa-
mous annual. In this—her eleventh
collection—she introduces, appraises
and interprets each story.

Edited by Judith Merril
A DELL BOOK 75c

If you cannot obtain copies of this title at your local bookseller, just send
the price (plus 10c per copy for handling and postage) to Dell Books, Box
2291, Grand Central Post Office, New York, N.Y. 10017. No postage or handling
charge is required on any order of five or more books.

The big shock-it-to-'em bestseller of 1968!

THE PRESIDENT'S PLANE IS MISSING

by Robert J. Serling

On a calm night in a nervous world, Air Force One jets off from Andrews Air Force Base. Aboard is the President of the United States, an idolized leader whose image combines the best qualities of John Kennedy and Lyndon Johnson—but whose inner thoughts remain a dark secret even to his closest aides.

The flight is normal—until the plane is high over Arizona. Then, suddenly, before a horrified controller's eyes, the plane vanishes from the radar screen . . .

"The shock of screaming headlines—a runaway bestseller that is tense . . . frightening . . . superb." —Kansas City Star

A DELL BOOK 95c

The most brilliantly
imaginative science fiction
novel since 2001 . . .

Logan's Run

by William F. Nolan and
George Clayton Johnson

Conceive of a time, hundreds of years from now, when
America is a technological Utopia. Society is led by a
computer system known as The Thinker. Sex is unlimited
and marriage is nonexistent. But there is a catch: no one
is allowed to live past the age of 21.

As a person is born in one of the state nurseries, a crystal
disk is embedded in his palm. At the end of his twenty-
first year of life the disk turns black, and he must then
give himself up for death. This is the story of Logan, a
man who runs from his own fate and remains alive as an
outcast.

"HIGH ADVENTURE" —Ray Bradbury

A DELL BOOK   75c

Soon to be a major MGM movie!

If you cannot obtain copies of this title at your local bookseller, just send
the price (plus 10c per copy for handling and postage) to Dell Books, Box 2291,
Grand Central Post Office, New York, N.Y. 10017. No postage or handling charge
is required on any order of five or more books.